THE BOY WHO RAN

THE BOY WHO RAN

Michael Selden

Woodland Park Press LLC
Woodland Park, Colorado

Woodland Park Press LLC
502 Fullview Avenue
Woodland Park, Colorado 80863

Cover art by Paola Sbriccoli

Cover and interior design by Belle Étoile Studios
Copyediting by Belle Étoile Studios
www.belleetoilestudios.com

First edition

ISBN 978-1-940640-00-6

Printed and bound in the United States of America

ACKNOWLEDGMENTS

I would like to acknowledge the contributions of the following people, in alphabetical order, who donated their time and efforts:

Stan Dains for his comments on early versions of the story.

John Hutter, who helped me by reviewing the story for both literary qualities as well as technical accuracy, especially on hunting and tracking.

Paola Sbriccoli, for her contributions and discussions on the story and for the cover art.

James Wolff, who provided a systematic read of at least two different versions of the book.

David Yoo for his developmental editing and great criticisms and suggestions on improving how the story would be told.

This book is dedicated to my mother and father,
both of whose lives were ended prematurely.

CONTENTS

THE BOY WHO RAN

PROLOGUE

The marauders crept quietly through the trees and tall grass, their attention focused on the prey—each man was cloaked in gray fur. The leader of the Wolf Pack carried a stone axe. It was a strange weapon that had been made by fusing several large flint shards into the leg bone of some beast, and was well suited for close-quarter fighting. The rest carried heavy spears, similar to the ones commonly used by hunters, but these men no longer hunted in the traditional sense.

It was dark; just a sliver of the summer moon peeked through the high, thin clouds to illuminate the ground. Within the pack's circle was a small nomadic camp. Ten hide shelters surrounded a fire that had been banked for the night, its coals still hot and ready to flare up with just a little more fuel and a little more air. One lone figure was visible in the camp. The sentinel leaned against a pile of hides; the man's chin, yielding to fatigue and the comfort of a full stomach, rested on his chest.

As the pack grew closer, the lingering aroma from the camp's last meal made their mouths water. A haunch of fresh bison was spitted but had been removed from the fire. A little away from the center of the camp was the treasure: A large cache of food had been painstakingly gathered and preserved over several hunts. It was packed and ready to be moved back to the camp's home village to the far north. This was the reason the others had come.

Something must have alerted the hunter on watch; he sat up quickly and climbed unsteadily to his feet—maybe he'd heard something.

What is that? he wondered, squinting into the darkness. It appeared to be a lump of rock where none had been before. Was this something new, or had he simply not noticed it before? The man took a few steps towards the trees to get a better look at the mysterious object, his spear grasped firmly in both hands. The hunter thought about calling an alarm, but imagined what the other hunters would say if he awakened the whole camp to look at a rock.

As the man drew closer, details began to resolve in the dim light. It almost looked like the rock was covered with … gray fur. Gray fur with eyes! He opened his mouth to yell, but rapid footsteps from behind made him pause for just one deadly moment. The last thought that passed through his mind was regret, not for himself but for his brothers, his mate, and his young son. An abruptly strangled cry was all that sounded when the multi-bladed axe cut through his neck; even that small noise triggered the predators into action.

Each ran to a shelter, ready to kill anyone who emerged through the low openings. Several of the awakened hunters, sensing danger, sprang from their respective shelters quickly and managed to evade the initial killing thrusts of the marauder's spears and began yelling to alert the others of the danger—but it was too late. As the mêlée took form, the voices of both defenders and attackers rose and blended in a chaotic roar. But the fight was not even and half of the defending men had been killed as they stepped through their low doorways. The pack leader ran to the last shelter, realizing that it had been left unguarded.

No one had come through the opening yet, but the man saw movement inside and then a figure framed within the doorway—it looked as though it might be a woman. *No matter,* he thought coldly, swinging his axe for the second time that night and striking the woman across the chest. The flint blades embedded into her ribs and the leader was forced to put his foot against the woman's side to pull his weapon free. The blades ripped her body open and she was pushed backwards into the shelter, falling. *This must have been the home of the sentry,* the leader thought, dismissing it as a source of further danger.

By the time the woman fell, just two of the defending men were still alive. A few of the women had joined their mates in battle to protect the children, but they were not a real challenge and died quickly.

Seeing that resistance from the defenders was over, the leader began howling, mimicking the sound of the animal from which his pack took its name. The other men copied the Alpha's voice and one by one entered the tents to murder the remaining women and the children. Two of the pack members threw fuel on the fire and then used flaming brands to set the shelters alight. The pack would burn everything to the ground and leave no one alive.

Inside the last burning shelter, the woman who had been wounded by the leader crawled painfully to the back of her home, a razor-sharp knife grasped in the crawling hand while the other was held across her chest. The boy was awake; his large eyes stared past her through the door of the shelter as she moved over him. He tried to speak, but the woman placed a bloodied hand over his mouth.

"You must be silent!" the woman commanded. There was a compelling, undeniable force in her whisper that the boy had never heard before. He couldn't imagine disobeying her.

The mother reached over his body, pausing with the knife over his chest as he stared into her eyes. Her hand hesitated there a moment but then continued past his body to cut a long vertical slit in the already-burning shelter. With a supreme effort, ignoring both pain and weakness, the woman rolled the boy onto her back, telling him to hold on.

The mother began crawling through the opening towards the edge of the forest. If she could reach the thick underbrush, maybe the boy could escape ... maybe he would live.

1

THE VILLAGE

The village was nestled between the western edge of the forest and the extreme eastern edge of the Great Plains. It was small; perhaps seventy or eighty people lived here. Twenty-four earthen mounds of various sizes and shapes were arranged in what seemed a haphazard configuration, but the position of each was carefully measured, dictated by tradition, and dependent on the status of the home's occupants. These were the winter dwellings of The People, the place they returned each fall to prepare for the frigid winds and snows of winter.

One shelter was much larger than the others. The Long Lodge was a gathering place for the community in the winter, a refuge from the cold where everyone could come together to share stories, conduct ceremonies, and celebrate important feasts. Sharing was essential when the frozen wind blew across the prairie and snow piled high around their homes; it helped them forget their hardships for a while.

Just north of the village, a small river emerged from the forest traveling roughly westward at a leisurely pace and along a seemingly undisciplined path. It was just an overgrown stream at this point, but its banks provided a nice place to take a nap under the shadow of the trees during the hottest days of late summer. People nearby drew comfort from its music as water rolled over smooth, worn stones and trickled into shallow pools. During the deepest parts of winter, the surface froze over with a thick crust of ice and the river's voice was muted. The People missed hearing its steady song in winter and listened for its return every day. The river always knew when spring was coming.

East of the village was the Great Forest, a mixture of old growth and new flowering trees interspaced with evergreens. It covered much of the Atlantic coastal region, the Great Lakes and Mississippi Basins, and the Tennessee and Ohio Valleys of what eventually, in six thousand years, would become the United States.

From here, the Great Plains stretched out to the west, an ocean of grass over subtle hills. Little groupings of trees were sprinkled here and there, lonely woodland castaways that seemed to have wandered off from the old forest. It was here at the edge, the place where the land transitioned from forest to rolling prairie, that the boy lived.

To people of the village, he was an unexceptional-looking boy, neither especially tall nor obviously talented. Few paid much attention to him if they thought of him at all. But the boy could move through the forest in a way that seemed almost magical—and he could run very, very fast.

For the boy, running was what was best in life. He sometimes ran across the wide-open pastures to the west, where even the wild animals might pause to look on at this strange human—to watch his lithe, smooth motion as he hurtled the rocks that seemed to grow from the soil. But it was in the woods where his talent was really special. He could run amazingly fast and in absolute silence through the densest forest without slowing. His body seemed to defy gravity as he slid between trees and through brush as though it were not there—a ghost. The boy saw and used his environment in three dimensions rather than the two that most people and animals perceived. This expanded vision provided him options the others didn't notice, and he was as comfortable ascending and moving along paths high in the trees as he was on the ground.

There was a freedom and joy in his stride that belied his demeanor in the village. Nothing in the world was better than to run; and there was no place as special to run as the forest. It was his greatest pleasure and could lift the weight of his long sorrow like nothing else. No one could run like the boy, and no one but the boy knew this—it was his most important secret.

2

RUN!

"It seems most of the boys have been asked to work on the harvest today," the hunter said. He was considering canceling the day's lesson. Only two boys had come for training, but the man knew that sometimes these smaller classes were more fun, and more useful. A small class meant he could spend time with each student.

"We will practice tracking anyway," the hunter decided, looking around for his mate. She was expecting a child, their first, and he had grown more protective of her since learning this under the midsummer moon.

Wild Flower was on the south side of the Long Lodge with her close friend, enjoying the sun and cracking dried nuts to make the cakes. She saw Red Sky looking for her and waved at him, knowing that he would look before leaving. The woman smiled inwardly at how much he had changed recently.

"Let's go," the hunter said at last. "I want to be back before the sun sets." The boys followed the man into the trees. He chose a path and they began looking for the signs of animals to track.

The boy had been following one of the many deer trails that crisscrossed their way through the forest during the early morning. This area was dense with undergrowth, shrubs, and bramble, all of which grew in the shade of the high canopy formed by well-spaced primordial trees. He almost smiled as he ran this morning; the earthy scent of the soil mixed in with decaying layers of plant material was comfortably familiar—home.

It would be good to visit a large sinkhole. The one he liked was well beyond the second line of hills and much farther than most people normally went. It was a good place to dive, a high rock wall that dropped into deep, still water. The sensation of falling was exhilarating, and he could swim to its tiny island where there might still be a few blueberries the birds and other animals had overlooked. A few of the cakes made from ground nuts and grains were in his pouch; blueberries would add sweetness to their otherwise bland flavor.

The sun was peeking between the branches of the trees that rushed backwards above him, its light created sparkling patterns that played along his skin. The moving bits of sun and shadow combined with coolness in the air to feed his thirst for more speed—he couldn't get enough speed today!

The animals, attuned to slight noises and subtle changes in the air, were often surprised as he passed closely by. He startled a bear but disappeared before the animal could decide if he was a threat, or even what to do. The bear looked in the direction from which the boy had come, saw nothing to cause alarm, and might have thought, *Strange human—invisible.*

The boy was invisible in the village too. No one looked at him the way he saw people looking at the other boys and girls, their sons and daughters and grandsons and granddaughters. No one looked at him with the smiling eyes and the warm expressions reserved for family. He didn't have a mother or a father or grandparents—or even a name of his own. He was just "the boy," a part of the background like a stone or a hide, tolerated but always alone and never really accepted.

This morning he was wearing an old deerskin breechclout, the castoff of another who had outgrown it. All of the boy's things were this way. He'd left his light tunic in the village today, since the weather was still good. In winter he wore long pants made from sewn skins and even wrapped his body in furs during the coldest months. Winters were severe on the plains and uncomfortable for everyone. The cold forced him to spend much of his time closed up in one shelter or another with different families; just thinking about the coming winter made the boy shudder.

Maybe the winter will be mild, he thought with a sigh. Last winter, a fearsome storm had all but buried the village in snow, and he was trapped inside for many days.

Never part of a particular lodge, the boy was passed from shelter to shelter to be warmed and fed. He remembered listening to a particular conversation between two women last winter—they didn't know he could hear them.

"It's your turn to look after the boy," Summer Wind said to Forest Water, the mate of the hunter Black Hoof. "We fed him and provided a place to stay for a whole moon and our shelter is smaller than yours. With the new little one coming, we need more space. Next spring, maybe we can enlarge the shelter, but it's winter and we are cramped. Will you please take the boy now?"

"But he's so strange," the woman replied. "I don't know if I can stand a whole moon with him always inside. The wind blows so hard sometimes these days that if he went outside he would be carried away. Why don't the elders assign him to a family?"

"I don't know, Forest Water. I'm not sure why but I wouldn't want to be the one stuck with him forever," the woman said. "My mate is already tired of him. He's always there! I know it's a hardship, but it's the same for all of us. Just take him. You don't need to do much—feed him, let him sleep in your shelter, and ignore him; you know how much he likes being alone."

The boy had heard many discussions of this sort during his years with The People. He tried not to think about it, but somehow the isolation made him want to be away and in the forest even more.

Strange? he wondered silently, tilting his head and remembering the women's words. *At least I don't argue and complain all winter.*

It wasn't always this way for him. He could remember a time when he was very small and he was not alone, when there was someone special for him too. There was one woman in particular who may have been his mother; that's how he thought of her. Then something terrible happened—something that he wouldn't, or couldn't, fully remember. Every time he tried, his stomach felt a cold chill and he would withdraw more deeply into himself.

At times the same recurring nightmare would awaken him and he would relive the last moments of his forgotten first life. Stubborn little flashes of memory and the absolute horror of its final moments were all that remained of his past, as if his current life began as the last one ended.

Who was *I?* he asked the forest again, hearing only more silence in return.

Certain impressions from those last moments were sharp and frozen in time. There was the smoke, and the fear, and the angry voices—images and sensations all broken up and scrambled, just like the sparkles of light that made their way through the trees. He remembered the woman crawling with him on her back, slowly, painfully, and in absolute silence. She had suffered some horrible injury and they were both soaked in her blood, but she refused to cry out or to make a noise at all. The woman carried him to the edge of this very same forest, many days' travel from where he now stood.

In the soft rustling of the leaves above, he could almost still hear her whispers that he would be safe in the forest. And if he chose to let the memory loose, he could still smell her fear, still feel the burning smoke in his eyes and lungs, and could still recall the never-to-be-forgotten scent of her fresh blood.

"You must be silent," she'd hissed, her mouth almost pressed against his ear. The woman was in agony but fighting to hide it; thinking back, he was sure now that she had been dying and was spending everything remaining of herself to save him. For some reason, he couldn't recall anything about her before that night, but her final words were carved into his mind—hushed and anxious, they retained undeniable power.

"Run!" she had said. "Run and do not stop!"

He had obeyed.

The boy had run and run, and run in the darkness, his feet bleeding and his skin torn by the thorns that clawed at him—unable to stop. A purpose had been ignited that night and it burned hot within him, driving him forward, hour after hour. He ran through the night and the next two days, pausing only for water as it found him. The boy had not stopped running until his small body, overcome by hunger and exhaustion, had finally failed and left him to rest on the cool floor of the forest. There had been a feverish awareness of deer—a mother and, especially, her fawn lying beside him for a time. They gave him warmth and a sense of comfort, but even now he wasn't sure if this had really happened or if it had just been a dream. He didn't know where his original home was then any more than he did today, but the experience of that last night remained fresh in his mind and was always with him.

The boy was approaching a low hill in the forest when a small movement caught his eye; something was ahead and to the right, just off the main trail— he was extra careful to be quiet. It was one of the other creatures of the forest. They fascinated him and he often thought of them as kindred spirits, even brothers. *Be very quiet,* he told himself, barely breathing.

Just a few steps from the trail stood an enormous buck, head erect and alert; eyes unblinking as his broad antlers turned slowly, scanning for danger. The buck sensed something, but the boy had been running as quietly as only he could. By chance, he had been downwind and his scent hadn't betrayed his presence.

"Hello, brother," the boy said.

The deer, looking for movement and shape, saw nothing, heard nothing, and scented nothing. He knew humans, knew what they looked like, how they smelled, and had felt the bite of their weapons before. But the branches and leaves of the brush broke up the boy's outline, obscuring his form.

This was not the first time that the boy had come so close to animals, but he was always interested in watching, following, and studying them. Many of the ways he moved through the forest had been learned watching different animals. Their competitions were even more fascinating to watch.

The trials between bucks in their season as they vied for the does were amazing. Every species had some equivalent. The boy had even watched the animals fight, for food, for territory, and for their lives. He recalled one fight in particular.

Two wolves had brought down a doe and were preparing to feed. The boy was high in a tree and had seen the end of the hunt, but the forest had other eyes too. A hungry wolverine had also witnessed the kill and was approaching it, showing no particular concern about the wolves. They were larger than the wolverine, and the boy wondered why it would risk challenging two such capable fighters. Why didn't it wait until they had their fill and then take whatever was left? But the wolverine arrogantly strolled towards the fresh meat as if they weren't there. The two wolves seemed confused and didn't immediately react, but both were ready to defend the kill—each stood defensively on either side of the doe's carcass.

Finally, one wolf expressed his objection to sharing with the newcomer, baring his fangs and laying his ears flat with a lowered head—and the wolverine attacked, but not head-on. It quickly stepped to the wolf's side, circling on its strong legs, and used its razor-sharp claws to strike the hindquarters of its adversary. The wolf yelped in pain and surprise, retreating from the doe and what had seemed a lesser opponent. The wolverine was unperturbed and approached the carcass again.

The second wolf wasn't having that! He probably wondered what his brother's problem was—after all they were wolves. He lunged forward. Once again, the wolverine stepped sideways—allowing the wolf to miss—and circled, marking this second wolf in the same way. This one was apparently a slow learner, because he needed a second lesson before understanding the situation.

Frustrated and bleeding, the two wolves retreated, offering little more than black looks and leaving the choicest parts of the doe to the wolverine. Maybe the wolves returned later for leftovers—the boy didn't stay to find out, but he remembered the lesson. The outcome of a fight did not always depend on which adversary was larger. The wolverine relied on superior intelligence and speed and knew the weak points of its opponents.

The young human harbored no illusions about life; hunting, competing, and defending your kill was the way of the forest. Even brothers fought for food—sometimes people even killed other people.

The boy was not a hunter, but knew that if he had a weapon now he could bring the buck down and provide food for the people of the village—if only he knew how. No one had taught him, and no one was teaching him to hunt or track the way they taught the other boys. He had never asked why—he didn't have to.

They don't really want me. The boy stared bitterly towards the buck, not really seeing him. *I can run faster than anyone in the village. I can get close enough to animals to touch them if I want. I can run all day and all night, but… what's the point? I have more in common with that buck than I do with the people of the village.*

He wasn't entirely comfortable with the thought of killing, even as he knew and accepted the realities of life. *Still, hunters are the most valued members of the village.* In the early years the boy believed it important to be closer to the people, but as he had grown older he was less certain and felt a kinship with the animals.

I have to eat, he argued. *I've tasted venison many times.* He knew that if he was willing to eat the meat from an animal then he should be willing to kill it as well. *I know I could kill for food, but I need to think about this some more and I need to learn. After all, I'm one of The People, not an animal… aren't I?*

The boy remained a while longer, watching the buck pull leaves from lower branches, and examining him more closely. This buck had a tuft of white hair on his left flank. It had an odd shape and was probably the result of some injury that had healed long ago. Its antlers were impressive, large and complex and almost twice as wide as the boy. He wondered how the deer could carry such heavy things on its head all of the time and tried to imagine something like them on his own head.

I think I'll call you White Flank, the boy said silently, naming the buck for its white scar. There was a wry expression on his face that gradually faded to something else as his mind wandered back to his unanswered question. A noise from somewhere behind caused the deer to flinch. Someone or something was moving along the trail from the west.

It sounds like a whole herd of bison, he told the deer silently, sighing. Then he heard faint voices. People were coming, but they were still far away.

The deer was aware of the people and decided that they were already too close. With barely a pause, the buck leapt over a large shrub and disappeared into the safety of the forest within just a few heartbeats.

Run, brother! the boy whispered silently. *Run, and do not stop!*

3

THE ACCIDENTAL
STUDENT

The boy decided to see who was following the trail, and he knew he would need better concealment. He chose a hiding place near the trail that was thick with underbrush and thorns, but which had a hollow center—almost like a little thorn shelter. Its "door" was a small gap close to the ground. He dropped low, his stomach almost touching the earth, to pass under the thorns and sharp branches to the shelter's heart. He could watch the people from here without being seen, just as he had watched White Flank. He didn't have to wait long before they arrived.

The noise came from three members of the village—two boys and Red Sky, the hunter with the unusual hair. His hairstyle was eccentric—even among the people, where styles could be quite elaborate. This man had cut his hair short and braided what remained on the right side but allowed it to grow long and free on the left. He claimed this was to keep it from interfering with the action of his throwing arm when he hunted. When asked why he didn't simply cut all his hair the same length, he said that he wanted people to know that he was a part of this village. Most members of the Eldest Village kept their hair long all year, while people from other villages often cut their hair short in the summer and let it grow back through the fall, winter, and early spring.

Red Sky was a great tracker and a very serious hunter, dedicated to constantly improving his skills—especially tracking. He was usually chosen to teach the young boys this skill. The boy liked Red Sky and felt that he understood him best. They were alike in an important way, each committed to perfection.

People of that era used a weapon called the atlatl to throw long arrow-like darts with great accuracy and distance. Each hunter carried one that had been constructed to fit his arm. Red Sky's atlatl was adorned with a beautifully carved bannerstone, used to adjust the way the weapon responded to his throw. Changing the stone's position was like tuning a musical instrument. His bannerstone was carved into the shape of an animal, a hunting talisman to bring luck in finding and killing game. The people had used this weapon for countless years. It allowed hunters to throw their darts much farther than they could thrust or throw a spear, using just their arm. They had traded away the spear's weight and thrusting force for the speed and range of the lighter darts. With practice and a sure arm, hunters could achieve phenomenal accuracy. The bow would not be used in North America for a few thousand years.

One of the boys traveling with Red Sky was named Morning Hawk. He was younger than but almost as tall as the boy and was the grandson of Great Storm, chief elder of the village. The boy liked Morning Hawk too; he was unusually friendly and had even shared with the boy fresh meat that had been cooked in a special way for Morning Hawk's grandfather.

The other person's name was Dark Sun. It was said that he had been born on a strange day when the sun turned black and the day into night. Dark Sun was a very different person than Morning Hawk, older and almost a hunter himself. He treated the boy as an unwanted irritation and sometimes teased him about having no one who cared for him. Dark Sun had also begun making demands of him to fetch wood or water, but usually he just ignored the strange boy, as did most people. The boy didn't like Dark Sun and avoided him when he could.

The boy didn't speak with either of them. In fact, he had not spoken at all since a hunting party had found him, more than seven years before. This set him apart and was one of the main reasons people thought him so strange. Most assumed he was slow, or maybe sick in some way. His silence isolated him almost as much as the time spent alone in the forest. He didn't know why he couldn't speak and had tried many times, but something inside always stopped him, even after he had finally understood their language.

The three travelers were each carrying an atlatl, already loosely fitted with a dart; they were obviously looking for game.

You won't find a deer, or anything else, if you keep making so much noise, the boy said silently. He wondered if the hunter had seen his tracks, but Red Sky gave no sign that he saw anything unusual on the ground as he passed where the boy had stood. The three walked by so closely that the boy imagined he could feel the heat from their bodies through the leaves, but they didn't look in his direction or show any sign that they knew he was there.

The hunter pointed at the disturbance in the leaves on the ground and the droppings that the buck had left. "Look at these signs," he whispered. "Imagine the size of the deer that left them. Dark Sun, would you say this is a buck or a doe, and how many summers do you think the deer has seen?"

From his hiding place, the boy frowned at the question. *How can someone tell so much about a deer from a few prints in the earth?*

Dark Sun paused before speaking. He had not expected to be tested but looked closely at the place where White Flank had been standing. He examined the traces—they were not as clear as they might have been. Leaves from many seasons still blanketed much of the space and detail was obscured, but there was enough information for him to assess the animal's size and tell if it was a doe or a buck.

Red Sky watched the older boy interpret the signs. His own reading had given him much more information than he'd requested, but he saw things the others would probably not consider. The teacher was planning to follow the buck and use its unusual signs in his training. Finding the tracks of this particular deer had been lucky and would make the lesson more useful.

"It's a buck, for sure. He seems to be big," Dark Sun ventured, "perhaps very big. I think eight seasons, maybe even more."

"Good. Yes, this is a buck and he may have as many as eight seasons, but I think he is slightly younger. My guess would be six to eight summers, and most likely seven. Notice how the track spreads with his weight and how the dewclaws make a deep impression, even when he is just standing still."

The boy was listening to everything and frowned more deeply. He wondered how much more he didn't see and what other things he needed to learn. Red Sky's words hinted at a whole new way to look at the world.

The hunter addressed his next question to the other boy. "Morning Hawk, how long do you think it has been since the buck left this place?"

The younger boy was nervous but wanted to show the hunter that he had listened during earlier lessons. "I am having trouble judging by the tracks, but the droppings are very fresh. I think it has been less than two hands since he left."

"Very good! I agree. The freshness of droppings is more important in this case since the tracks are not clear. Based on the scrapes in the earth, I believe he was here for as much as a hand of time and I think he left less than a hand before we arrived, maybe less than two fingers."

A hand referred to the basic unit of time people used to describe duration. When a person holds a hand out at arm's length and bends the wrist so that the palm is held towards his face, the distance across the width of the four fingers on the hand covers an angle in the sky when viewed from one eye. One hand is the time it takes for the sun to travel across the sky the same distance, or angle, as the width across the four fingers held together. One hand is about one hour; the width across one finger would be about fifteen minutes.

Red Sky decided to move on. He wanted to follow the trail of the buck and use different signs along the way for his impromptu class. He knew they would find imprints that were more pronounced and examples of other spoor that would be useful for the lesson.

The boy stayed with the small hunting party, just as he sometimes followed animals in the forest; he wanted to watch and learn, realizing that the other two boys were being trained to track today. He knew now that this "hunt" was really a teaching exercise.

While moving along a path parallel with the small class, the boy was sometimes compelled to ascend to the first canopy layer of branches in the trees, so that he could get close enough to see and hear what was said. He noted how the boys moved, and he frowned at their carelessness.

Red Sky was much quieter than the two boys, but not quiet by the boy's standards. Occasionally, even the hunter stepped on a thin root or dry branch that snapped its warning to the animals—for them it would be a deafening alarm. He tried to hear as much as he could, focusing intently on what the hunter was saying. The man was showing them what to look for, teaching them how to recognize clues that revealed something about the animal being tracked. The man even hinted that they could track a particular deer over a large distance using unique signs left by that individual animal.

I didn't know that you could track a specific animal just from its signs, the boy said silently. This day was opening a whole new world of possibilities, and it was also giving him an idea for the future.

The class moved as Red Sky spoke, following the hunter as he tracked the buck.

"The hunter needs to envision where and how the deer is running, learn the way it prefers to move. Look at the little signs along the way. Look for the signs that you can easily see and the ones you cannot but that you know must be there nonetheless.

"Is the buck moving in a straight line, or is he wandering and looking for food?" the hunter continued. "If he is wandering, you should move slowly, as he may also be preparing to rest. If he is running in a straight line, move quickly. Follow the disturbance in the brush and try to see as the buck must have seen, when he was deciding how to move. If you can visualize what the deer sees in your mind and can imagine how he might have run, then you will find it easier to follow him through the forest. It's important to learn how he thinks. When you are able to track him even as you run, then you will know that you are becoming a real tracker. If you can track quickly then you can follow the buck quickly, maybe quickly enough to catch up to him."

The hunter showed the boys other useful things—the fragments of hair left by the buck as he brushed against a tree or through shrubs, places where the deer's antlers disturbed foliage above the ground, and the choices the buck made when moving through foliage. "The deer knows which spaces will allow his antlers to pass and which won't," the hunter said.

The boy was absorbing as much as he could.

Red Sky also dissected the unique tracks left by the buck. As always, there were four imprints, one for each foot with aligned impressions. The rear hooves and front hooves of a deer normally struck closely in line on the ground—this pattern was consistent, depending on the stride being used. White Flank was different.

The man stooped over a flat area that was relatively free of leaves, pointing out the characteristic imprints left by White Flank. "As in the clearing, you can see how much wider the front hooves are than the rear hooves—the rear imprints are closer together than the front imprints. That proves he is a buck; his chest is much broader than the width of his flank. This is a large buck. See, even the back legs are widely spaced and he makes deep imprints in the soil, even as his hoof spreads under the weight. This soil is packed, so he is very heavy—maybe the largest I've tracked. But it's also important to understand the hardness of the ground when gauging the buck's size. But this," he said, pointing, "is why I chose this set of tracks for our lesson today."

"Do you see how the left rear hoof seems to strike at a slight angle, and how it often strikes differently and is not consistent and not in line?"

Morning Hawk and the boy in his tree both nodded.

"This buck has had an injury to the left rear leg at some time in the past. He is not injured now and is able to move fast; see how his stride is well spaced when running? Also, he does not tire easily and has run for a great distance. We can use this information to identify and follow him. There may well be other bucks that have suffered a leg injury, but each will show a distinctive pattern."

Dark Sun must have thought he was too old for this lesson since he looked around and played with his atlatl, his attention wandering. He had come along mostly to accompany Morning Hawk— befriending the younger boy gave him an excuse to be near Hawk's older sister.

Even from his perch in the tree, the boy could see that the hunter was aware of the older boy's rudeness, but the man chose to say nothing.

Red Sky concluded his lesson, saying that the buck was far away now and that they should return home. "The tracks are getting older as we go on. I think that we are more than a hand, almost two hands, behind the buck now, much farther behind than when we started. He is moving quickly. Maybe we will cross paths with this buck again someday. I think we will know him."

The boy was grateful for the opportunity to have watched and learned, and he hoped to do something like this again soon. There seemed to be many interesting things to learn. It would be exciting to watch an actual hunt where Red Sky tracked and brought down a buck.

After the others left, the boy returned to each of the places Red Sky had stopped to describe different signs. He examined them more closely and tried to visualize how a deer might run, just as Red Sky had said. He hadn't realized it was possible to track a particular deer, but now he saw exactly what the hunter had been describing. The left rear leg, the one with the white fur pattern from a scar, did not strike the ground the same way the other hooves did. The weight was uneven and the angle of the hoof was slightly askew. He saw how a hunter might use a mixture of things to follow a deer, and he wished that Red Sky could train him too.

After the boy had reviewed the lessons and understood every sign the man had pointed out, he decided to run to the top of the great hill. It dominated the forest and was visible from far across the plains. Climbing it often helped him think. Not tired at all, he also wanted to look past the trees and across the grasslands to see if there were bison running nearby. The lesson had given him new energy and now he craved the release of running hard.

From the top of the hill, the boy could see his entire world. To the east, the forest rose and fell over the smaller hills and across valleys. Rocky out-growths peered through the foliage here and there, like the bones of the world exposed through soil and undergrowth and trees. Details melted together as he looked farther away until the forest became a soft green blanket, as if cast over the hills by some giant. When he looked even farther, he could almost see the mountains rising in the distant east.

Immediately below him, trees covered the nearby valleys, hiding their mysteries beneath multiple layers of canopy. Everything was still green since fall had not yet arrived. Each morning these valleys filled with a fog that reminded him of thick smoke, but didn't burn his eyes. The boy especially liked to run through the early mist when the dense air swal-lowed even the tiny sounds he might have made. Morning was the time he was able to forget every-thing for a while. This afternoon he was struggling. He needed to decide what to do.

Am I one of The People or am I something else? It was a question he had asked many times, never really expecting a reply. Intuitively, he knew that only he could provide the answer.

The village was to the west, where the trees ended. It looked so tiny and fragile from here, a speck of humanity built on the edge of the vastness of the plains. Beyond, the grasslands stretched out farther than the boy could see.

He'd heard about the enormous herds of bison that grazed and wandered wherever the grass or their interest took them. The boy could see a few animals running free and wondered what it would be like to live as the bison lived. It would be exhilarating to run with them, a part of the herd and a part of the endless land—no past and no thought for the future. There were no horses for the boy to watch. Horses had been extinct in North America for three or four thousand years and would not return until the Spanish brought them back to the New World.

The boy had been going back and forth since the lesson—truthfully, much longer than that—trying to decide. Now he chose.

I want to learn to be a hunter; I want to be one of The People.

The boy never took a decision lightly. Once he decided that he would do a thing then he would do it with all of himself, allowing nothing to stop him.

There was a lot to learn and he would need a teacher, or teachers. After the elders, hunters were the most respected people in the village. One was at the heart of every family; they belonged with the people and to the people.

Learning to do something took commitment and a lot of hard work. The boy had discovered that when he wanted to learn to do something well, it was best to keep his mind focused on one thing at a time. Watching Red Sky teach the boys had given him an idea. He wanted to see what he could learn from the hunters, secretly at first. When it was time he would find a teacher … somehow.

4

THE SECRET STUDENT

If the people noticed a sudden change in the boy's behavior, they showed no obvious sign of it—certainly no one said anything to him. Most either didn't see him or pretended not to. He had been staying at White Buffalo's lodge for some days. It wasn't his favorite place—the man just ignored him, but his mate didn't bother to hide her unhappiness—the boy tried to make himself as small as he could. His favorite lodge was Four Bears', whose mate always tried to make the boy feel as though he was a part of the family. Both of their children treated him well too.

After the experience of Red Sky's lesson, the boy spent weeks following different hunters as they taught the boys the hunting skills that would be needed. He wanted to watch and to learn without being seen, just as he had done that first day. Later at night, he listened carefully to the men talk as they planned the next day's activities, and in the morning he got up well before the sun to make his way to wherever the training would be. He'd find a good place to wait for the hunter and his students to pass by. Sometimes he waited in the forest but other times he was forced to go southwest, among the rocky knolls that bordered the plains. Each day he tried to learn something new. It wasn't easy to be a good hunter. It required skill and knowledge, patience, a persistent toughness, and the willingness to do what was needed without hesitation.

Not all boys were ready for every lesson; the hunter in charge of training for that day decided who would go. Those not ready stayed in the village. Usually the hunter spoke with the boys' mothers and they were assigned some other task for the day. This spared hurt feelings; there would be other opportunities for them to learn.

The hunter Raven was sharp-eyed and more observant than most. He noticed the boy watching as he was teaching the hand signs used during group hunts. It was a surprise to see the boy paying so much attention to anything. Raven had often asked himself what went on in the boy's head, wondering if maybe he could learn to communicate using the hand gestures of their ancestors.

It was a language even older than the village. Relatively few signs were all that remained of what had been a subtle and complex language. Most had been slowly forgotten over the millennia as their use declined. Raven knew more of the signs than any of the other hunters and had a good grasp of their sense, but even he knew only a small part of the original language.

During group hunts, the men often waited far apart from one another, hiding but still needing to communicate. When the bison thundered between them, the men couldn't hear one another and the signs helped them to coordinate their movements. Raven decided this would probably be a bad time to attempt to teach the boy, but later this winter he would try.

One night, the boy heard about a unique opportunity to learn. An event was being planned for the near future. Most of the village was gathered around the fire that evening, although the night was still warm and they were spread out, away from the fire's heat. He was sitting by himself at the edge of the gathering, partially in the shadow of a lodge. It seemed no one noticed how attentively he was listening to the plan.

The full moon was already high in the sky, and its light painted the prairie to the west in a silver cast. The long grass was still tonight, and there was no breeze in the village. Moonlight couldn't penetrate the forest, but the boy could see that the trees on the largest hill were swaying. He knew that the wind was sometimes like a river, its currents flowing as though contained within unseen banks. Tonight it flowed high above the ground while the village rested in its still shallows. He wished he were up there now to feel the wind flow over his body, but wanted to hear the teaching plans for the next day and had picked up a hint of this other event.

Morning Song watched the boy gaze high into the trees, wondering if she'd really seen him earlier. She had been waiting to meet Squirrel; they were going to try to catch a fish in the stream, just like the boys had done the previous day. Squirrel said that she was sure they could do it too.

Song had watched as five of the boys followed Red Sky into the forest. Each carried a small amount of food to last the day. While waiting, she noticed a witch-hazel shrub near the point where the stream passed out from under the trees and decided to collect some of its branches. Her mother made a medicine by boiling the leaves and bark stripped from the stems together. She had asked Song to look out for the plant.

While she was stooped over, cutting the branches with her knife, the girl thought that she saw something move very fast, high above the ground. When she turned her head, a figure was hurtling through the air between two trees. It looked like the strange boy, the one who stayed with them from time to time. Song blinked and wiped her eyes to make sure she wasn't imagining it, but he was still there. The boy had stopped and was squatting on a large branch, looking down into the forest near the place where the other boys had gone. She stared at him with her mouth open; he was perched impossibly high in a tree. The girl was about to yell at him to be careful when Squirrel arrived and drew her attention. When she looked back, the boy was gone.

"Did you see that?" she asked.

Squirrel looked where she pointed, a playful smile was in her eyes. "See what?"

"You know, the boy, the silent one, the one who never talks. He was flying through the trees! Did you see him?"

"Stop playing with me, Song. There's nothing there." The younger girl was laughing. "Do you have visions of the strange one very often?" Squirrel asked, laughing so hard now that she needed to kneel down. "If you're going to daydream about a boy," she said between gasps, "please choose one worth your attention, one who acts like a human at least." Morning Song was a little offended at first, but soon she joined in the laughter.

"Well, I thought I saw him, anyway. Let's catch that fish."

Now, watching him as the hunters spoke, she couldn't help notice how intently he focused on what they said. There was intelligence in his eyes that seemed out of place. The girl frowned, and wondered if everyone had been wrong about him. And what the boy really thought of them all. Few of the others were kind and some were deliberately mean to him. Dark Sun in particular sometimes went out of his way to tease him and had even pushed the boy down once, when the adults weren't watching.

The boy never seemed to pay much attention to people; it was as if he lived in another world, and that somehow their cruelty couldn't touch him—now Morning Song wasn't so sure.

Another set of eyes had been watching the boy too. Dark Sun noticed the way Morning Song looked at the strange one, mistaking her curiosity for something more. He couldn't imagine why anyone like her would show the slightest interest in the boy, who was never asked to do anything and couldn't even speak. She was still looking at him even now! Why? Dark Sun had gone out of his way to be friendly with her and had even made friends with her brother Morning Hawk, but Song paid little attention to him. He cast a black look at the boy now, frowning.

That night, the hunters talked about an unusually late hunting trip this year. Great Storm had decided that more meat would be needed for winter and that a hunting party would cross into the open prairie soon. It was to be a short journey; only the men would go this time. Most of the village was still collecting late-summer nuts and grains and preserving them for storage. The chief elder didn't want this important work interrupted. The harvest had been good and the work to preserve everything was taking longer than expected, but another hunt was needed. There was still time and no need to hurry, but Great Storm didn't want to delay its start for long—it was always difficult to know precisely when the weather would change, even for an elder.

The journey would also offer an opportunity for the hunters to test two of the oldest boys who seemed ready for their first group hunt. The men had told Great Storm that the two had passed the other tests. By tradition, formal participation in a group hunt marked the all-important transition from boy to hunter. The men would continue to watch the two ahead of the hunt. They would decide if it was time for the boys' trial, and for them to take more responsibility in the community. The final judgment would depend on how they performed during the hunt. Gray Wolf would lead; he was the most experienced hunter in the village. The elders said that they would announce the day the journey would begin by the next night.

In the meantime, there was still training to be done—the teaching would continue until the hunt began.

"Running Stag, I want you to gather the other boys and meet me near the fire tomorrow morning," a hunter said to one of the two hunter candidates.

"Where will we go, Laughing Bear?"

"First we will practice throwing at the targets and then we will visit a place to the south. There are a large number of rabbits past Kneeling Rock. I want to see how everyone does with living, moving targets," he said, laughing. A number of the other men chuckled as well. It was one thing to throw at a static target or at a grass wheel rolling in a predictable way, and quite another to hit an animal on the run—especially a rabbit, which frequently changed its direction very quickly.

The boys and men alike regularly practiced throwing darts. There was an area set aside for this near the village. The men and boys practiced to improve their accuracy from various distances, both at set targets and at woven grass wheels, which were rolled by other hunters to simulate an animal running. A low hill behind the target area ensured that the darts would only strike the ground if the thrower missed.

The boy didn't have an atlatl, but he thought it might be possible to make one. There was one hunter in particular who was known to be skilled at making and repairing weapons.

Maybe I can learn how to make an atlatl properly if I watch him, the boy thought.

The men and the two candidates waited impatiently for the big hunt, but the boy stayed focused on his plan and rigorously continued to follow the different classes. In addition to basic skills directly related to the hunt, the teachers also explained other important things a hunter needed to know: How to determine when it was acceptable to kill a doe; what time of day one might find different animals near a watering hole; or the differences between hunting a bear versus a deer. In each lesson, the teacher always emphasized the importance of the clean kill. Laughing Bear summed up The People's philosophy on the matter the day the boys hunted rabbits. One of the boys had stopped chasing a wounded animal that managed to get away.

"We are all children of this world. When we hunt and kill for food it's a part of life, just as being born and growing old is a part of life. How we treat one another is important, not only our brothers and sisters in the village but all of the children, human and animal. We are a part of the world in which we live, not separate. It is wrong—an insult to our brothers and our ancestors—to cause more pain than necessary. This is how we behave because it's how we would want to be treated if we were the hunted. Kill, but kill cleanly. If you make a mistake and only wound the animal, then it is your responsibility to correct that mistake."

The negligent student was required to track down the wounded rabbit, and was not allowed to give up or to speak for three days, or until the animal had been found and released from its pain. Wounding and abandoning an animal was considered a serious offense and could bring bad luck to the village.

Morning Song had been watching the boy more closely whenever possible through the days leading up to the hunt. She still wasn't sure about what she had seen in the trees that day, but increasingly she noticed little things about him. These were things she had never paid attention to before, like the way he walked. The boy normally moved slowly and seemed almost clumsy when he walked about the village, but she'd seen him dodge Wild Flower when the woman was walking backwards and not looking where she was going as she was carrying a large hide with another woman. There was no hint of clumsiness about his movement then, and the girl wondered how he had gotten out of the way at all. It bothered her that she had never noticed these kinds of things about him before. She decided to ask her mother about him.

"Mother, the strange boy, the one who never talks, how did he come to be here and who are his people?"

Singing Water looked at her daughter, wondering what was spurring a sudden interest in the boy. "He came to us years ago, when you were much younger. The hunters had found him far away to the north, but I think there's something wrong with him." The mother looked at the frown on the girl's face. "Don't worry, Song, he'll be fine. There's nothing you can do—he's not right in the head, but we will always take care of him." Unlike many of the other women, her mother never complained when it was their turn to host the boy; she seemed to feel sorry for him and always asked that her family pretend that he was a part of their hearth when he stayed with them. The girl smiled back at her mother, but didn't say more.

The boy followed every hunter when he was teaching the other boys, but he especially liked to listen to Red Sky. There was so much more about the animals to learn than he thought possible. A skilled tracker understood both the physical characteristics of the animals, as well as the behavioral habits of each species. The best hunters knew how their prey lived, what the animals liked, and they tried to think as the prey might think.

A class was following the trail of a bear one day. Red Sky had chosen a different student to lead every so often. That boy was required to walk with the hunter and decide where the class would go next, explaining what he saw and why he chose a particular path. Early Sparrow was leading when the bear's tracks suddenly vanished. The signs were old and faded, and the tracks would have been difficult to follow even under ideal conditions—these had been washed out by rain. Now the signs were not clear. Sparrow stopped, seeming to be at a loss for what to do next.

"Where did the tracks go?" Sparrow wondered aloud, still thinking.

"Remember that the tracks are only a part of the picture," Red Sky reminded the boy. "Look ahead at where the bear was going and think back to places we've been that are similar to this—what choices did the bear make those other times?" There was another period of silence as the hunter waited for the boy to think before prodding more. "If you were a bear, what would be the best direction to move? As yourself, where do you think he was heading?"

"I . . . I don't know. He may be heading for the water, but there are at least two paths that go in that general direction," Sparrow said.

"Remember, the bear can easily go over obstacles, or he can pass under them, but it's not as easy for him to do both at the same time. Which direction favors his particular size and the way he has shown that he likes to move?"

"The left," Sparrow said, deciding finally. "He could pass under the leaning tree easily, whereas the right-hand path needs a complex mixture of high and low movements. He could get by, but the way would be harder."

"Then let's follow the left-hand path and look for signs. We can always return here if we are wrong."

A while after taking the path on the left, the group found more tracks that had survived the rain.

The particular hunter teaching the class changed every day, or every few days. The hunter chosen depended on the specific skills being taught. Some hunters were more knowledgeable about particular game and others about specific skills. Every teacher brought something unique to the class. Laughing Bear was best with an atlatl, accurate and unbelievably fast. He was able to load and cast darts quickly and with deadly effectiveness—even small animals like rabbits had virtually no chance once he'd seen them.

The boy thought back, remembering Laughing Bear's words during the lesson.

"Realize that the weapon is a part of your arm, an extension of yourself and not something separate," the hunter had said. "If you have practiced enough, you won't need to think about the throw, you will

just place the dart on the target—as fast as thought."
The hunter had demonstrated how one could load
and launch multiple darts in different directions.
Each of his darts had hit the center of every target.
"Practice, practice, and practice. Change your target's size and distance often, and vary the way you
stand and the angle from which you throw just as
often. Do this until you don't think you can do it
one more time, and then do it some more. When
it feels as natural to load and throw as it does to
walk or to breathe, then you are getting closer to
understanding your weapon. Tomorrow we will go
through different techniques when you use other
kinds of projectiles, like multiple stones or lighter-
weight darts."

During lessons, each of the hunters was careful to
describe what he was doing and why he was doing
it as shown. The teachers didn't just do something
and expect the students to guess what was happening. Some of the lessons focused on other things,
like what to do when something unexpected happened—including emergencies, such as if they were
injured or lost. Every aspect of what was needed to
survive was important.

Only when all of the senior hunters unanimously
agreed that a boy was ready would he be tested. It
was important that every hunter accept a boy before
he became a hunter. Only a hunter could form a family in the village; this was one of The People's most
important traditions. The requirements to become
a hunter went well beyond measuring if a person
could track and kill an animal. The men needed to

trust that the new member of their brotherhood was ready. Their lives depended on each hunter's ability and judgment. If the men didn't know how the candidate might behave in a stressful situation, then they wouldn't want to be paired with him during a dangerous group hunt.

The more the boy followed and listened to the teachers, the more he wondered why it had taken him so long to understand how important everything was, and to realize that he should have made a much stronger commitment to the village years before.

The men were patient with the boys and understanding when they made mistakes. Training was the time in which the boys were allowed and even expected to make mistakes. Mistakes helped to drive the lessons home, even more than the boys' successes did. Seeing the men and women's patience and the care they showed when working with the other children was a lesson for the boy too. Something cold and hard and distant inside of the boy was beginning to soften and he grew to accept that most the isolation he'd experienced was his own fault.

Morning Hawk hesitated before speaking openly in front of his parents. He approached Morning Song by the river. His older sister had always looked out for him and he didn't want to embarrass her. As a healer, their mother was often called to help with the birth of a baby or to treat a serious wound, and during their mother's long absences Song had been like a second mother to him. So instead of questioning her in front of their mother, as he had been advised to do, he chose to speak with her privately.

"Song," he began uneasily.

"Um-hum, what is it, Hawk?"

"Is it true that you ... like the silent one? Someone told me that you were watching him closely." Morning Song wondered who would have noticed, or even cared, if she were looking at the boy, but she also understood the focus of her brother's question and smiled at him.

"No, Hawk, not the way I think that you mean. I was just wondering about him, where he came from and how he wound up here. I feel sorry for the boy."

Morning Hawk's frown faded as he listened. "Well, Dark Sun seems to think that you look at him a little too much. But I understand now."

Morning Song didn't say more. It sounded as though Dark Sun may be just a little too interested in what she did. He was a couple of years older than her, but he was known for having a bad temper. Song was remembering that Dark Sun liked to pick on the boy. It might not be healthy for him if Dark Sun thought she liked the strange quiet boy. She decided to be more careful as she watched him, looking for the little inconsistencies she'd noticed before. And it wouldn't help him if other people also mistook her curiosity for more. Morning Song was sure the boy was hiding something about himself, but maybe, at least for a while, it would be better if she seemed to ignore him.

The training for the boys was kept at a rigorous pace throughout the time leading up to the late-summer hunt. Much of this training still occurred in the forest, because of the variety of animals and the diverse terrain it offered. Here, the boys could learn more about plants too, which ones could be used as medicine, which were edible, and which were dangerous. Four Bears was the most knowledgeable hunter on the use of plants. He'd learned a lot from his mate, Singing Water, but sometimes she led lessons too.

Basic healing was important to know, since the hunters needed to be able to treat wounds while far away from the village—at least well enough to get the wounded hunter home. When the men went hunting on the plains at least one of them carried a kit that Singing Water prepared for them. It contained plants to help stop bleeding and an assortment of materials to bind wounds, or to hold a broken limb in place. Singing Water showed them how to splint a broken leg using leather straps in the kit and wood that they could find in the wild. This would hold it in place until they could reach her or another healer to have the limb set. Under normal circumstances, a healer would travel with the hunters, but there were times—such as the upcoming late summer hunt—when they might be many days from help.

The class was sometimes conducted near the village, either to allow the boys to practice with weapons, or to learn from other teachers, like Singing Water. There were many important skills to learn. The women were far more adept at processing the carcasses of animals for meat and other useful materials—tendons for cord, bladders to hold water, and hides for clothing and shelters. They knew how to work the hides into skins or supple furs without damaging them. Although work was often divided by gender, between men's work and women's work, people understood the value in knowing something about everything; too much specialization among a small community is dangerous.

At times the hunters would choose one of the candidates for a special test. A lone hunter, or perhaps two, would take him into the forest to let him demonstrate what he had learned. The men allowed the boy being tested to lead the hunt and to bring down larger game. They would also ask him questions—testing his knowledge in many different areas. These tests were used to see how well the boy had learned everything, and to measure his character under stress. It determined if he was ready for a group hunt, and to assume his place as a hunter in the village. There were currently eight boys in formal training—nine if the boy were to be counted. People didn't think of him as a normal child, or even a member of the community. And just as the boy hadn't fully appreciated the value of working closely within the community, the people didn't understand how much value they were missing in the boy—like his intelligence and strength of character, even more than his unique skills.

The boy always followed when the others were being trained, staying as close as possible to the class. He was often perched high above them, masked by lower canopies of branches in the forest. After each day's lesson, he would go back and practice what he'd learned, again and again—the boy was never satisfied with anything less than perfection from himself. Sometimes he went alone deep into the forest to practice where he wouldn't be seen or interrupted. The boy especially liked the subtleties of tracking different animals and even conducted pretend hunts.

While the forest was a useful school, there were other lessons better learned on the plains. Group skills in particular were vital when hunting bison. These coordinated hunts allowed the men to harvest a number of the animals at one time and let them accumulate enough meat over the hunting season for the village's needs. During group hunts, the men worked together as a team. Hunting bison in their massive herds alone was far too dangerous, but as a team they more than evened the odds. The group hunt practice sessions were some of the most important lessons offered, but they were also much more difficult for the boy to follow. One or two hunters would play the role of the bison during the exercises, wearing hides and acting like bison. The others would pretend to hunt them, setting traps and running across the prairie while using hand signs to coordinate their actions.

The boy felt exposed on the plains during these pretend hunts, despite the tall grass. He was usually forced to watch from a much greater distance than usual—sometimes very far away, where he could see little and hear less. Although the tall grass was everywhere, and seemed to promise many useful places to hide, the hunting classes moved across great distances and covered large areas. The class was usually spread out and there was no way for the boy to be near a teacher.

The boy knew team skills were key to his plan. The forest brought variety to their diet and provided many materials that the village needed, but nothing could replace the large quantity of meat, the enormous hides, and the other products that the bison hunts brought. During group hunts the men were close to the giant beasts; their safety depended on precise coordination and knowledge of what each man would do—there was little room for error. Not being able to practice these skills left a gaping hole in the boy's training, and he knew it.

The boy hoped that during this late-summer hunt he could witness the group tactics put into practical use for the first time. He had always traveled with the people when they made their annual pilgrimage across the plains, but he had never actually watched the men during their hunts. This time would be different.

5

THE GROUP HUNT

The men would be hunting bison. The large beasts dominated the Great Plains with their uncountable numbers, and their enormous humps often towered over even the tall hunters. The boy wondered how the men, armed with only an atlatl and its slender darts, could bring down the bison without being trampled by the herd. He knew the hunters had done it before, but knowing was not the same as seeing.

It would be a short hunting trip, and the last chance this summer to add large quantities of meat to the village reserves. The men were traveling light but were still expected to harvest at least a dozen bison. Great Storm wanted to be prepared for a winter as severe as the last one had been. Winter had lingered well into the spring and forced the elders to impose a strict rationing discipline. Everyone remembered the experience and no one wanted to repeat it.

The boy was determined to follow the men but knew that he needed to be careful. It was important that he not be detected until it was too late to send him away. The night before the journey he gathered a few things that would be needed. There was a small water bladder and a basket that he slung across one shoulder. In the basket were his tunic and some food. The food consisted of chewy dried meat, pemmican—an intestinal casing filled with a mixture heavy in rendered fat—and a number of the cakes that were a staple for the people. It was a hunter's diet. Pemmican, especially, provided the concentrated energy needed to fuel bodies under hard use. The men always carried it when they traveled fast, and it could be eaten even as they ran. The boy wasn't sure how long the journey would last, but he carried enough food to last at least half a moon's time. He was so anxious to get started that he had trouble sleeping and was up long before even rumor of the sun's light had touched the highest clouds. Although he'd sensed no one stirring in the village yet, the boy took a last look over his shoulder to make sure that he wasn't spotted leaving. He ran quickly to an outcrop of rocks to the southwest, below the point where the little river that passed the village joined with a larger river flowing from the north. It had gathered and combined the waters from many streams like theirs and would continue to grow as it snaked west and south. Eventually it would become a great river that emptied into the Gulf, far beyond where anyone from the village had ever traveled. The boy planned to wait here for the men to pass. The hunters always followed this path when they were heading for the open prairie to the west. There was a ford here—a place where the river was shallow and wide and easily crossed. The men would normally go directly west to pick up the tracks of bison herds. They would be moving fast this time, without the very young and old to slow them down. The two oldest boys were coming too; the hunters had deemed them ready for the challenge of their test.

The boy stayed hidden behind a rock he had chosen the day before, carefully peeking out around its side every now and then as he stretched his arms and wiggled his legs to help keep them awake. He had been too excited to sleep more than a little during the night, and had awakened every so often. Finally, he heard a young voice drifting through the morning air.

"I'm going to try to bring down three bison," the voice was saying. The boy knew the voice belonged to Dark Sun, even without looking. The older hunters didn't say anything. They walked in loose groups of three and four. Each man carried his weapons and a kind of pack made from a basket slung over one shoulder, just like the boy's. An older hunter, Gray Wolf, was near the front. His eyes were glued to the horizon, and there was an inscrutable expression on his face. The man nodded to let Dark Sun know that he had been heard but otherwise didn't respond—a hundred things were on his mind this morning. Dark Sun glanced at the older hunter's face and stopped talking.

After the men had passed, the boy stayed in his hiding place another two fingers before following.

The sun was just peeking over the southern edge of the large hill to the east as he began to follow the men west. The sun's brightness helped hide the boy during the morning. To see him, the hunters had to look directly back into the rising sun as it crested the hill. The blinding light provided a kind of bright camouflage in the early morning, but as the sun rose higher, the boy knew that he would have to rely on the tall grass or use scattered trees and rocky outcrops to the north and south of their path to avoid being seen.

Visual obstacles screened him from the men through most of the day, and he stayed far enough away so that any noise made was not loud enough for them to hear. The men weren't expecting anyone to follow them, and this helped a lot. It was rare for one of the hunters to look back towards the forest, but for some reason Raven did, just as the boy was moving behind a group of rocks.

It looked to Raven as though a figure was dashing across their trail, and the man hurried ahead to where Gray Wolf was walking.

"I think someone or something may be following us," the hunter warned.

Gray Wolf halted and looked back to where Raven was pointing. The whole hunting party stopped and several of the men wanted to know what was happening.

"Raven thinks he saw something on our trail. It could have been anything, but just in case it's a predator, Raven and White Buffalo, will you investigate?" Both men nodded. "I don't want to be surprised while we sleep. Catch up with us when you've made sure." The two men headed back along the path together, their weapons ready.

The boy had seen the men stop and point to where he had been just a short while before. He was always careful to step on ground that was already disturbed, but he knew that his tracks might still be visible if the men looked at the right place. For now, he crouched behind a low rock, well south of the men's path.

Two of the hunters ran back and seemed to be looking for tracks, but the signs were confused and the boy's steps light. They paused momentarily where he had changed direction, then turned their heads left and right uncertainly. Had Red Sky been with them, he might have seen more, but after looking for a finger of time the men hurried back to rejoin the hunting party.

That was close, the boy thought to himself. *I need to be more careful!*

He remained in his hiding place a long time. Nearly being caught had made him nervous, but he also didn't want to lose track of the hunting party. If he were discovered the men would probably order him back to the village, and he knew that he would have no choice but to obey. However, if they didn't know he was there they couldn't give the order. He guessed that there would be some point beyond which he would be allowed to stay, even if discovered. His goal had been to remain hidden until the hunt was over and then reveal himself. He bit his lower lip, thinking about that last step.

As he shadowed the hunters that day, he frequently found it necessary to run at a diagonal with respect to the direction the men walked. This meant that the boy traveled much farther than the hunters, snaking his way back and forth across their trail to remain screened from view. This was especially true when they hit patches of terrain where the grass was short. It also forced him to increase the distance between himself and the men, and he was nervous that he might miss it if they changed direction while he was too far away to notice.

That first night, he found a safe and reasonably comfortable place to sleep. It was near enough to the camp to see the fire in the distance, but far enough away that they wouldn't be able to hear or see him. The grass on the plains was so long in some places that the boy occasionally wondered if he would need anything else to hide behind. It sometimes grew as tall as him, but there were also places where he felt very exposed.

The men were being very careful with their fire—it would be easy for it to get out of control. Fires in the tall grass could spread rapidly and were one of the greatest dangers the men faced. The nights were still warm enough that a fire was often not necessary, although towards the early morning the air temperature became cool and made the boy shiver. He wore his tunic to sleep and used his small flint knife to cut handfuls of the long grass to use for padding and insulation, and these kept him warm enough.

The boy needn't have worried about missing it when the men changed direction. The hunters found what they had been looking for during the middle of the third day. It was obvious. Ahead of them, the tall grass suddenly disappeared and the ground looked bare. The boy couldn't imagine how many bison it would take to do this to the land. As far as he could see to the west, the earth had been trampled, its grasses cut down to nubs in order to feed the herd, and what wasn't cut short had been laid flat under millions of hooves. It was easy to see which way the herd had gone. Now, it would just be a matter of catching up with them and then devising a plan for the hunt based on the terrain they found.

The hunters increased their pace to a slow jog now that the goal was clear. The boy thought that they might have some idea about how far ahead the herd was and might be adjusting their speed to catch up at the right time of day. He knew that the men's attention would be on the bison now and he could move a little closer without great risk of being noticed. His water skin, which had last been filled at a stream two days before, was gurgling from the space inside. The boy didn't know how many days they would need to travel, or where the next water might be, but he was determined to see the hunt through to its conclusion. He planned to help the hunters after the killing, when the long, hard work began—if the men let him.

The boy knew that both Dark Sun and Running Stag were a part of the hunt and wished that he were with the hunters too, able to hear the men talk. But he also knew that the men would not have allowed him to come, either because of his age, which was almost enough, or more likely because of his strangeness. It was possible that the hunters still might demand that he return to the village when they saw him, but once a hunt was over there were never enough hands to do the work of cleaning and skinning the animals and then drying the meat.

They'll let me stay if I am helpful, he guessed. *But I need to stay hidden until after the hunt.*

Everyone slept in the open at the end of each day—the weather was still fine and there was no reason to erect a shelter. The men had not brought complete shelters anyway, just some of the older hides to transport the meat. Shelters were heavy and would have reduced the amount of meat that could be carried home. The boy watched the men's fire through most of the early part of each night until he drifted into uneasy dreams.

In last night's dream, he imagined that he was sleeping in a hide shelter. Someone was with him, but he wasn't sure who it might be. Something was different—there was a familiar presence and a woman humming a tune he hadn't remembered ever hearing until now. He knew this was a memory of his mother and also that it had to be a dream; no one sang to him any longer. The dream felt better than the life he had now, but there was still that sense of foreboding; the boy knew what was coming next and waited with his stomach clenched.

He heard the shout, and then another and another until finally the sounds joined, rising to become an ugly roar, uncounted voices shouting in anger, some in pain. Even asleep, the boy knew this was more than just another dream; it was more detailed than his previous dreams. His mother moved to the door, a shadow in the opening of the shelter. Just then something hit the tent hard and he heard the woman grunt in pain, falling—soon everything began to burn. He could feel the warmth of the fire now—it was hot! He awakened suddenly with a jolt, panting heavily and his hair wet.

The sun had completely risen in the east and the day was already warm. This was much later than he usually slept, and he was afraid that the men might already have left. Carefully peering over the rock that had served as a headboard last night confirmed that the camp was empty. The men were not in sight, but the boy didn't panic. He could still run faster than the men would be moving, and they were all following the path of the bison anyway. If he ran south he should see them before long. The sun was still in the east, to the left, as he ran. He wasn't worried about being sighted at this point; everyone's attention would be fastened on the southern horizon, looking for the herd.

A few strips of dried meat, a dry cake, and a mouthful of warm water to wash everything down constituted his breakfast. The water was more than half gone now, and he knew he would need to find a stream or a clean pool to refill it sometime today, or at latest tomorrow morning. Despite carefully managing how much he allowed himself, he still needed to drink something, and it looked to be another warm day. He removed his tunic.

At last, he was running. Initially he was just stretching his legs to work the sleep from his body. The stiffness of having slept on rock would dissolve as his muscles warmed up. After a short time he began to really run. It felt good to fly across the open plains, free of cares and with an endless horizon. This is how he always imagined the bison must feel when they ran.

The humidity was higher than it had been the past few days, and his sweat stayed with him. Wind blew from across the flat land to the west where the bison had been, and tiny bits of straw-like grass clung to his skin, making him look and feel like one of the seed cakes he carried. But he didn't mind; the hunt was getting closer.

Before the sun had moved two fingers across the sky, the men came into view. They were to the west and still moving south, tiny figures just on the edge of the horizon. The hunters must have started well before dawn to make this much progress. There was a small group of trees on the horizon too, directly south, and the boy veered slightly east. He planned to allow the trees to come between the men and himself. The others were running too, but not fast. Their pace looked as though it were measured for a long day. It didn't matter to the boy—he could run all day too—but the harder he ran, the sooner he would need to find water.

When the sun had reached its highest point in the sky, the men slowed and then paused. The boy looked farther south and saw what had stopped them. Ahead, the plains seemed alive. The land was dark with their numbers, a rippling cover of deep brown fur stretched beyond sight, extending to the south and the west. It was an enormous herd, so large that the boy could not see its end. The bison went on forever and, from his perspective, the herd appeared larger than the plains themselves—even bigger than the forest! How could there be so many animals? How could they survive? He had never seen anything like it and didn't know there were that many animals in the whole world!

Gray Wolf stopped the men to sample the wind and discuss how they would hunt the bison. They were looking for a group that could be separated from the main herd and one that was not too large. It would be tricky. If the main herd was spooked and ran in the wrong direction, the hunters could easily be trampled without ever having been noticed. This had happened before. Gray Wolf had lost his son in a bison hunt almost seven seasons before. It had been a terrible time for him. The hunt was successful, but that was no consolation for a grieving father.

He was more cautious than many of the younger hunters now—not so cautious that he wouldn't take measured chances, but determined to make sure that the men returned safely to their families too. Some of the less experienced men tended to be reckless. The young often think that they will live forever, that they are invincible. Older hunters know better.

Conditions looked good. The older man could see a group of bison that was promising; a small part of the unthinkably large herd had wandered to the east and was lagging behind. They were just west of a group of trees and moving slowly to the southeast. The hunters might be able to use the trees to isolate them from the main herd. The animals were seeking grass that had not yet been mowed down by their brothers and cousins and uncles and aunts—at the center of the herd pickings could be pretty slim. East of the small copse, the grass looked long and tender. It was time to act.

The hunting party moved quickly eastward, around and through the trees, preparing to set their trap. Gray Wolf had a plan and was directing the hunters.

"We will form two main groups for the killing. Laughing Bear, lead your group to the southeast, stay low, and be prepared to turn the small herd north if necessary. I will take another group east. Dark Sun, you go with Laughing Bear's group. Running Stag, stay with me. Use your hides for cover and, when necessary, to frighten the bison. Four Bears and Raven, it will be your job to separate the little herd and get them moving east, once they pass the edge of the wood. White Buffalo, give each group's leader some of the coals from last night's fire, in case the main herd turns east and fire becomes necessary—but be very careful! We don't want an uncontrolled burn to start. Do you all know what to do?" The men nodded—they were experienced, and the boys would each be paired with a seasoned hunter.

"Your first duty is to make sure that all return home safely—every hunter should have a partner in case someone falls. Save the hunter first. Here is where I want everyone." Gray Wolf drew the plan in the dirt, pointing to where different groups of hunters would be with respect to the trees, and stressed again that safety was the most important thing. Finally, the old hunter paused to address Dark Sun and Running Stag separately. "There are many bison; just look to the west if you doubt me. But we are only a few hunters and the village depends on us." Then he turned to the leaders.

"Let's move."

The boy saw the men turn east to follow the herd that had gone around the group of trees where he had stopped. This was good luck for him because he would be close to the hunt and able to see everything clearly. At first he was afraid the men might see him, but the small wood he was in offered a number of safe hiding spots. The boy saw that he would have the best view from high in one of the cottonwood trees on the southeast corner of the woods. He also knew, because of the trees, that there was water here.

The men moved out from the small woods and arrayed themselves into two main groups across the plains, southeast of the woods. Two men headed farther east to head off strays. Each of the groups formed a rough line along the path where the men would drive the bison; the hunters were teamed up in pairs. The plan depended on being able to isolate the small herd from the rest of the bison on the east side of the small wood, but sometimes plans went wrong. The larger herd could turn east; the men were too few to turn them and most would be trampled. The small herd could suddenly turn north or south together and overwhelm the men on one side. Any number of things could go wrong, but the men were experienced and prepared to adapt as the situation unfolded.

The stray herd had wandered to the east, but it had still not passed the trees. This gave the men the time needed to deploy and to stop moving, concealed beneath the small buffalo skins they each carried. If the men moved openly, the buffalo would probably spook and the opportunity would be lost.

The boy saw the men, draped in their hides and bent over, running to the east to form up two lines. The hunters settled to the south and the north of where the bison would be driven. Two of the men hid in the woods, just at the point where a gap was forming between the small herd they would hunt and the much larger main herd. They waited patiently, looking for the right moment to separate the small group and get them moving faster to the east.

One of the two men signaled when the herd seemed safely beyond the woods and then the two beaters ran south into the gap, waving their hides over their heads and yelling loudly. The animals were confused and began moving faster, away from the disturbance and from the main herd. They loped eastward between the two lines of concealed hunters. This is when the boy saw how it worked.

The men erupted from their concealment and loosed a coordinated barrage of darts—and the bison began to fall. One by one the hunters struck down the wild animals, throwing as they stood beside the moving herd, and then running in parallel with the bison to stay in range. Most darts found their target quickly but a couple only wounded the animals, and these latter bison tried to escape to the east. The two hunters assigned to head them off were waiting for them and dispatched the strays using their atlatls. Once the animals were all down, the men retrieved their long thrusting spears before approaching the fallen beasts, ready to speed an animal's death if necessary.

The main herd to the west was disturbed by the activity and moved off in the opposite direction, but it was not a stampede. It had been exciting to watch, and the boy was impressed by the two men assigned to move the bison along. They had run directly towards and among the herd, seemingly without fear—and the bison were so big and strong.

He remembered when one buffalo had veered away from its eastward track and had run directly towards the hunters to the south. The men on that side focused their efforts on this animal and brought it down before it could harm anyone. To be a hunter was to be a brother, and the men took responsibility for the lives of all their brothers.

The boy squatted on his branch, watching the action, imagining how he might be able to run swiftly up beside a bison and thrust a spear into its heart, then dance away before it could turn. He didn't realize the strength it took to pierce the hide and penetrate the ribs. His ignorance was forgivable given his lack of training and experience.

When the bison were finally all dead, the hunters gathered in a group to celebrate the success of the hunt—no one had been hurt. After a short time, the men chose one of the animals and opened it to taste the liver with gall, bile taken from the gall bladder. Dark Sun and Running Stag were each given a choice piece for their part in the kill.

Now came the hard part. Some of the men used their knives to begin the process of cleaning the animals, while others started gathering materials to build the line of fires that would dry the meat and produce the smoke that kept insects away and helped preserve everything. The boy knew that the men would be coming to his woods in search of fuel for the fires. When on the plains, the men mostly burned sod or buffalo excrement, but if wood was available it was used first.

The boy knew that the time had come to let the men know he was here. This had always been a part of his plan. Helping would allow him to watch everything more closely, and he hoped the men would begin to know him for something other than an almost-welcome stranger. He collected wood nearby to help with the fires. Then, taking a deep breath, he stepped out of the copse of trees and walked towards the hunters. Raven was the first to see him and pointed him out to the others. Everyone looked surprised, even shocked. One man actually seemed afraid for some reason. Did he think that the boy was a spirit? Gray Wolf approached him, and Dark Sun drifted closer to listen.

"Boy, did you follow us from the village?"

The boy nodded that he had.

"Why? Did you want to watch the hunt?"

Again, the boy nodded but looked uncomfortable.

Gray Wolf wondered if the boy was hungry, but he didn't seem to be suffering and had already collected firewood for the work ahead. The older man hadn't expected the boy to be here, nor did he imagine that the boy would think about the work to be done, but it was clear that he wanted to help. *Well,* Gray Wolf thought, *we may as well let him.* He wondered if the boy was really as slow as everyone said and decided that he would watch him until they returned to the village. Despite his silence, the youngster might be brighter than everyone thought. Certainly it couldn't have been easy to follow the hunting party so far and then to appear in just the right spot at just the right time, ready to help. The boy should have been far behind the hunters.

Dark Sun looked agitated and spoke to the hunter. "Why don't you send him back to the village?

He wasn't invited. Is he going to be rewarded for disobedience?"

Gray Wolf looked thoughtfully at Dark Sun for a moment, saying nothing at first. It was a look that made the new hunter feel that he should have kept his thoughts to himself.

"I do not think the very hard work we are all about to do is reward, but if it were, then I'd like to reward more people because as many hands as possible are needed now." He said this with a smile and then his expression changed to that of the teacher. "A leader needs to consider what is best for the hunt and for the men. I do not believe the boy was disobedient; we didn't tell him to stay in the village." It was only a mild rebuke. Gray Wolf knew that the question had been spurred by unwarranted jealousy, but it would only make matters worse if he spoke more strongly.

Dark Sun looked down as he heard the reply. Gray Wolf was right about the hard work, but the young hunter still didn't like the strange one and had always resented the liberties the boy was allowed. However, he knew better than to say more.

The boy gathered more wood for the fires and, afterwards, helped the men carry water from a small stream near the woods. Gray Wolf had seen more seasons than he liked to admit, but he felt young with the success of the hunt. He waved the boy over to one of the bison to show him how to skin and clean the animal. The man helped remove the hide and then cut strips of meat for drying. Afterwards, the boy continued collecting more wood to burn in the fires. Gray Wolf nodded his approval.

The fires were built in lines, across the direction of the wind. They helped to quickly dry the meat, and smoke from the fires kept the insects away as it cured. The meat was cut into narrow strips and draped over hastily fashioned racks above the fires or on cords strung between poles set deeply into the ground downwind. It was like drying the wash while adding a smoke seasoning that also helped to preserve the meat.

Normally, they would have had many more hands to help. The women of the village in particular had more experience with certain tasks and normally took responsibility for this work. It was also the women who worked the hides, scraping and preparing them for the making of winter clothes and shelters, but the processing of animals was a group activity involving the whole village. Large hunts required that the people be able to move fast and work hard. About half of the people would normally go on the hunt from wherever the village was camped. But today the men would have to make do.

During the nomadic months of the year, there was a home camp where the elders, children, and a few others stayed. A second, mobile camp followed the herds from a relatively safe distance. This temporary camp would be located much closer to the herd so that everyone could help after the bison had been felled. Often there were several hunts not far from the home camp, and the mobile camp would move frequently. Sometimes there were several hunts in one area and the people kept many fires burning. After days of shifting from kill to kill and processing the game in an area, they would collect back at the main camp to pack everything up and follow the herds across the plains.

People used long poles to drag the meat and new hides back to their home. A pole drag, or travois, was a kind of reverse wheelbarrow—without the wheels. For this hunt, the hides would simply be folded and bound with leather cords for the trip back, then placed on old worn or damaged hides, used with the pole drags to hold the meat. The women could work the hides back in the village, but the meat needed to be dried quickly.

The boy stayed with Gray Wolf through the next days as the work was completed. The older hunter showed the boy what to do and then watched. He didn't speak, but the man noticed that he seemed to learn quickly and was surprised. Most of the people said the boy was slow and dull-witted since he never spoke, but Gray Wolf knew that speaking was often overrated. He wanted to discuss the boy with the elders when they returned home. It would be a terrible waste for the village not to train the boy properly, even if he didn't speak.

"Boy, have you ever hunted?" he asked.

The boy shook his head.

The man frowned. He should have received some training by this age—something wasn't right. Gray Wolf was older now, nearing the time when he would hunt less. If necessary and if the elders agreed, he might take the time to teach the boy himself. Some of the others might not want to waste the effort on him, as they saw it. But his time was his own to waste. It might not be possible to include the boy in the normal lessons, but he could be trained. After his own son had been killed, his mate had died giving birth to what would have been his daughter. These past years, Gray Wolf ate with his younger brother's family but still lived alone in his own shelter. He had not taken a second mate out of respect and grief for his lost family. The hunter thought that he could train the boy and wondered how much he knew already.

The people had found the boy years before. A group of hunters following a deer trail had come across the boy lying on the ground. He was asleep and it looked like he had not eaten for days. The leader of the group believed that the boy had seen fewer than six summers at the time. There were cuts along his body, probably from the thorns that seemed to grow along every trail. When the boy sensed the men were there, he jumped up and looked as though he would run away. The men looked so big and they carried spears and knives and other weapons, but they didn't look unfriendly, so he stood still and waited.

They spoke to him in a language that he didn't understand, although he did recognize many of the words. The boy stood silently, waiting for what they would do to him. The leader offered him some food from a basket he was carrying across his back. The meat was dry and chewy and the boy thought it was the best thing he ever tasted. The hunters were far north of their village. Several of the men were carrying game slung between them on long poles. The leader signaled that the boy should follow and he nodded that he understood.

Life in the village had been different for him, different than his already-fading memories of the other village, but the boy was grateful to the people. He was not sure how far he had run but knew he was very far from his old home. There was no reason to go back; this was his new home now.

Some of the women and a few of the men tried to speak with him. At first he didn't understand them, but their meaning was clear from their expressions and the gestures they made. The boy still said nothing. Something always kept him from speaking. It wasn't that he didn't like the people. They were very kind to him. It was something else; something inside of him kept him silent, kept him from even trying to speak. It was a strong compulsion that, unfortunately, grew into a bad habit.

During the hunt the boy had watched the hunters finish off one of the last bison. The long darts had severely weakened but not killed him. One of the hunters used a long spear with a heavy stone point and thrust it into the side of the animal, just behind the shoulder. It was done to be merciful and for the safety of those who would need to dress the game, but it gave the boy an idea. This was a kind of weapon he could use even now! A hunter on the run, one who could get close to the animals, might be able use something like it. A fast hunter might be able to thrust a lighter version of the spear into a deer or a boar while running. The boy wanted to learn more about this weapon. It appeared to be easily made, assuming one had a stone point. The boy also wanted to learn to use the atlatl, but he thought the spear would be quicker for him to master.

It was fortunate for him that he'd worked with Gray Wolf, who was also the village's master weapon maker. He hoped the man would allow him to learn something about the making of weapons, but of course, the boy couldn't ask directly. The older man was patient and didn't treat him like a pariah. It felt strange...good, being treated like a person—as though he had some value.

The meat was dried, the skins had been scraped to an extent and then wrapped into bundles and bound—they were ready to leave. The boy worked extra hard helping the men drag the meat and hides back to the village. Everyone was working harder than normal and even Dark Sun was glad that the boy was along to help pull the pole drags.

When the hunting party arrived back in the village, the story of how the boy had appeared from the small wood was listened to in near disbelief. The people hadn't even realized that the boy was gone. Had they noticed his absence, the last thing they would have thought was that he was with the hunting party.

The boy had helped drag one of the large bundles of meat over the past several days and was tired. He knelt down for a moment to rest, still staring at the ground, and when he lifted his head he found himself staring into the curious eyes of Morning

Song. She had been staring at him the whole time as he pulled the pole drag into the village. The boy noticed a difference in the way she was looking at him. Normally, girls in the village either didn't pay attention to him at all, or if they did look, it was to tease one another about who would be his mate. This girl wasn't looking at him like that. Hers was a welcoming, almost familiar look that he might have expected a friend to share. But then the moment passed and she looked away.

The village elders listened to Gray Wolf's story as he described the hunt, and they also listened to his thoughts on the boy. Great Storm wore his characteristic taciturn expression as he thought about what he had heard. He remembered the day the boy had been brought home to the village quite clearly. The people didn't know what had happened to the boy's village; the elders had sent runners out to other villages to learn what they could and to find the boy's parents.

Much later, they learned about the destruction of what they assumed was the boy's home. It was the first time they had heard of men attacking and killing everyone. The elders presumed that the purpose was to steal food, but it might have been a grudge of some kind—the wholesale massacre of a village was an extreme response, an unthinkable act.

It bothered the elder that they seemed to have failed the boy. He had never been formally adopted. At first they had thought it important that the boy go back to his own people, but after a time the situation set into a pattern—a bad one. They had tried speaking with him, wanting to learn his name so that something of the lost people would remain. They felt it would be wrong to impose a new name of their own on him; it seemed important that he keep something of his past—the name was all that might be left. But no one had ever come for the boy and by the time they learned the truth, it was too late. Bad habits are harder to break as time passes. No one seemed to want him, no one would speak for him, and the elders had failed in their duty. They hadn't pressed the issue. He would be a perpetual, silent stranger.

But the past was the past. Great Storm saw an opportunity to correct their mistakes now. If Gray Wolf saw something useful in the boy then this might work out for the best. It could solve two concerns of the elders at once. The boy might gain a permanent guardian, a father, and Gray Wolf would have the boy on which to focus his attention.

The elders might have assigned a new mate to the man, but they hadn't done so out of consideration. Gray Wolf was the most respected hunter in the village. Most people assumed he was destined to become an elder someday.

The three old men discussed the matter that night and in the morning summoned Gray Wolf to give their approval. It was decided. Gray Wolf should try to train the strange boy.

"See what the boy can do," he advised privately. "It would be a waste of his life if he never improves."

Gray Wolf nodded his acceptance and said that he would do his best.

6

THE TEACHER

The day after returning to the village, the boy was asked to join Gray Wolf where he was working. The man was repairing darts for the other hunters, replacing the fletching on some and the stone tips on others. In some cases a dart's shaft was damaged and he knew that he would need to make a whole new dart.

Shafts for the darts were made using wood harvested from specific kinds of trees and then straightened using steam and pressure. Gray Wolf also made his own glue from the hides of the bison. Together with strong fiber-like strands, the glue held the different parts of the weapons together. The fiber was taken from sinew, strong deer tendon that had been pounded and separated into strands. This was wrapped around the fletching and points before the glue was applied. Sharp points were bound to the tips of the darts and spears. These were made through a process of chipping and pressure-flaking certain kinds of stones into precise shapes. The man found good stones nearby; there was a certain part of the river where they were abundant. They could be shaped in a predictable way, and held a sharp edge. He could shape them using several different techniques. The old hunter made or found all of the materials he used to fabricate the weapons. He was a methodical craftsman and did his work with painstaking care.

"I'd like you to help me with this," the man offered. He had not looked up from his work, but directed a quick furtive glance at the boy to see his reaction. The boy's eyes widened and his face lit up in anticipation. Gray Wolf allowed himself to relax. He wanted to show the boy that there were skills, other than hunting, that were needed by the village. At the same time, he wanted to test the boy's aptitude for detailed work—the crafting of weapons required attention and patience.

The boy stood to the side of where the man was working, ready to help. Gray Wolf nodded to him and gestured that he should sit, aware that the boy was watching his every movement.

There was a kind of box made of wood and old hides from which steam was escaping. This was held over a large hide pot that was filled with water and suspended over a fire. The water kept the hide from burning; it was important to monitor the water level. Another similar container was nearby, this one much smaller. It held a thickened substance that was kept warm and in a liquid state by the same hot water. The man began talking as he worked.

"It is important that the shafts of the darts be very straight. Steam relaxes the wood and allows me to bend it without breaking. If I bend it this way, the wood will keep the shape I want. The shafts are made from different kinds of wood of useful length that I find in the forest, but they all need to be straightened. I usually do this in two stages since the wood can also sometimes bend due to stress as we work it.

"Once the shafts are reasonably straight, I use a knife to get a cross-section that is generally round, then I use stones of different roughness to work the shafts until they are round and smooth. This stone," he said, lifting one of his tools, "is very rough and it allows me to remove a lot more material than some of the other stones do. I scrape it along a shaft until the wood is very close in shape to what I want, and then I use a stone that is less rough to smooth the wood. Finally, a much finer stone is employed to remove very small splinters and to make the shaft feel perfect. If necessary, we can use the steam again to make the shaft as straight as possible, rolling it along a flat rock to check that it is ready. There is a stack of roughly shaped shafts over there," the man said, pointing at a pile of thin wooden rods.

The boy picked up one of the rough shafts, his face serious. It was perfectly straight and rounded. If the boy placed one end on the ground, the other end would come to his shoulders when he was standing, and it was about as thick as one of Gray Wolf's fingers.

"I want you to take these two stones—this is a medium-rough stone and the other is a finishing stone. Let me show you what to do." The man showed the boy how to use the stone to shave just a bit more wood from the shaft until it was much smoother and closer to the final shape. "See how smooth this is?"

The boy nodded as he felt the difference.

The man then demonstrated using the fine finishing stone to achieve a product that was ready. "Do you think you can do the same thing with these other shafts?"

The boy nodded.

While he was working on the shafts, the man attached feather fletching to some that were already finished. "I'm attaching these using this sticky substance that the fire is keeping warm for me. When the glue cools it will be hard. To make the feathers stay in place, we will wrap a bit of this thin fiber around here and tie it off. Later, I'll show you how to attach a stone point using the same process. Soon, we will make stone points together—that's probably the hardest part of making a dart.

"The feathers I am attaching help make the darts fly true, but they need to be tightly bound so that they don't come loose and change the dart's direction or make it lose speed."

"We use many of the same techniques and tools when we make an atlatl, but in that case we need to bend parts of the weapon to make it hold the dart. Some weapons have a much larger platform. Those are used to throw stones rather than darts and are more useful when hunting birds. They allow a hunter to throw several stones at the same time, or one dart. Usually only one of the stones will strike the bird." The man continued to attach fletching until he had a collection of about twenty shafts that were ready for points.

"See these stone points? I normally make them from quartz, and I can make the stone take whatever shape I want by carefully removing tiny pieces at a time, just like the shafts of wood. The correct shape is a narrow, sharp blade that can cut through the hide of a bison without breaking. This platform on the bottom provides a way to attach the point to the shaft of the dart." The man continued to explain how the darts were put together as he worked. They were of varying sizes and thickness. Most darts were much longer than the arrows that would later be used with bows, perhaps twice as long.

Gray Wolf used flint for some of his points and for knives, but good flint was often difficult to find. The People had been developing techniques to make excellent sharp points from other rocks, like quartz, for a long time. Any stone that could be predictably shaped through impact, using a hammerstone, and by using flaking or grinding techniques, was acceptable. The points Gray Wolf made recently resembled a modern Christmas tree; the base, or stand, of the tree was used to attach the point to the shaft. Archaeologists would call it a "Stanly point" one day, named after a county in North Carolina where they were first excavated.

The older man watched the boy from the corner of his eye, trying not to be obvious about it. The boy's concentration was exceptional. He never seemed to tire, never lost patience. The man had demonstrated several different techniques and had asked the boy to try each one. Every time the boy quickly grasped what he was taught and was able to copy the technique perfectly. Later, the boy even managed to make a complete dart, attaching one of the points Gray Wolf provided. He was not fast, but his work was of good, or even exceptional, quality. By the time they were done, the sun was setting.

Unusual, the man thought, reflecting on the boy's work. Most boys would have rushed through one or another process, and he would have asked them to rework the dart. But the boy's work was flawless. *He will be a good craftsman,* the man concluded. *How could we have missed these qualities all of these years?*

Each day after the midday meal he spent several hours with the boy, teaching and watching, sometimes even learning something. The boy picked up new skills very quickly and was even able to improve on a few of the techniques he saw demonstrated. Next, Gray Wolf taught the boy how to make an atlatl and even helped the boy fashion his own first weapon. They fit it with a simple, unadorned bannerstone. The shape carved into a bannerstone wouldn't be chosen until the boy was a hunter and the people knew more about his character.

As the boy sat with the man, many sets of eyes were keeping track of his progress. Silver Dawn was curious about him. She had never tried to speak with him, as Gray Wolf had done. For years, she had paid little attention to the boy, except when it was their turn to take care of him. Until now, she would have said that the boy was more than half animal, never speaking, and barely responding—he had reminded her of another child born to the village when she was a young girl. That one hadn't lived past his eighth summer. She had just assumed that the boy would always be the same way, but Gray Wolf said he was intelligent. *Who knew?* She was watching the two of them now. It made her happy to see that the older man, her mate's brother, had found such an apt pupil.

Morning Song tried not to look. She knew that she was being watched closely and didn't want to make Dark Sun dislike the boy even more. Still, she managed to look at him secretly now and then, watching as he learned to make weapons. When the boy had returned from the hunt, everyone else was stunned. She had been relieved.

The girl had noticed the first night that the boy was gone. She'd watched him during the preceding days, how closely he paid attention to the hunters. When he didn't return for several days, she hoped he was with the men, but had also been worried that he might be hurt somewhere in the forest. She pointed out his absence to her mother as they were grinding seeds and grains for the cakes.

"Mother, I haven't seen the quiet one for days. Do you think something might have happened to him?"

Her mother looked at her carefully. "You seem to have taken an interest in the boy lately."

She smiled at her mother as though she had told a joke, rolling her eyes impatiently. "I'm just trying to be aware of people, mother. I want to be a healer someday too and thought that a healer would want to be aware of those in the village who are not the strongest, those who seem helpless." Her comment seemed to assuage her mother's concern.

"I don't know, Song. Sometimes he disappears for days. I guess that someday he may simply not return, and that is sad to think about. I've gotten used to seeing him, and since he's lived here we've mostly had good luck. The sick and broken ones usually don't survive long, but he's surprised me. He seems healthy enough, just strange in the head."

The day after making the boy's atlatl, the man began teaching the boy how to throw accurately. They used targets made of old hides bound to poles. After three afternoons of concerted, almost obsessive practice, the boy was able to hit the target near its center eight times out of ten. His face had fallen in disappointment when he missed its center that first day. Most boys would have been delighted to hit the target at all.

The boy noticed that Dark Sun, who was now a hunter, had also chosen to practice on the throwing range at the same time and seemed to watch him a lot. The new hunter made him nervous—he wasn't sure why.

The next step in his training was to translate his accuracy at close range to longer distances. It would be almost a moon before Gray Wolf would allow the boy to try to kill an animal, but they had made a good start. For the man, it had been surprising how quickly the boy learned the subtle nuances of the weapon. It was not an easy weapon to master since both the atlatl and the dart flexed and changed under the stress of being thrown, but he never stopped trying. Such intensity and concentration was almost unnatural in the young ones.

The man continued speaking to him as if they were having a conversation, although of course the boy never answered, but then he also never complained. Gray Wolf chuckled at the unexpected benefits of a student who didn't speak. The boy showed a lot of promise and might one day be a very good hunter—if only he could talk.

There was one issue that continued to irritate the man. The boy still disappeared for hands of time every day, mostly during the early morning. Sometimes Gray Wolf would see him come from the forest and at other times from the plains. The man frowned at this seemingly fatal flaw in an otherwise good student; it spoke of an uncharacteristic selfishness—it was one of the things that had kept the boy apart for years.

"What does he do all morning?" he would wonder aloud. By late afternoon his doubts were eased, mainly because of the boy's single-mindedness about everything he learned. Other than these two matters—the lack of speech and the hours of absence—the boy was a model student.

One afternoon, after having gauged the boy's progress, the man asked him a question.

"Would you like to hunt with me tomorrow?"

The boy's eyes widened—the delight in his face was easy to read and he nodded yes quickly.

"We will need to leave together early in the morning. Please make sure you are here and ready to go around dawn." Again, the boy nodded that he understood. The hunter wanted to get to a watering place frequented by different animals before the day was very hot.

Dark Sun heard the man invite the boy for a hunt and was furious. It had been more than a year after he started training with the atlatl before he was invited on a hunt. And, Gray Wolf never took boys out singly; the man had never spent much time with any of the others—boys far more worthy and able to speak. He couldn't understand why Morning Song and now Gray Wolf paid so much attention to him. Dark Sun felt his body shaking just thinking about it and fought the urge to confront the boy—to put him in his place. Why didn't other people see how perverse it was to train this thing? Who would want to hunt with him?

After he had spoken with Morning Hawk about his sister's sudden interest in the boy, he hoped that Hawk's mother would stop Song from having anything to do with him. But Morning Hawk had spoken to the girl rather than the mother. The more he thought about it, the more Dark Sun knew that he had to do something and thought it ironic that it might bring trouble to himself, just for doing what was right. He needed to find the boy alone, maybe in the forest, to privately force some reasoning into the simpleton's mind. To him, the boy wasn't much more than an animal, although the young hunter never asked himself if he would be angry if Song was simply interested in studying an animal.

Despite his worry that the boy wouldn't be ready, Gray Wolf found him waiting just outside of his shelter when he got up. The two shared breakfast under a late moon before leaving. The glow from the sun behind the hill let just enough light through the leaves to illuminate their path. Each carried an atlatl, several darts, and their knives. Gray Wolf handed a small bag of food and a water skin to the boy. The man also carried his long spear, just in case.

"I want you to watch today; the next time we go you will take the lead."

Once they were in the forest, Gray Wolf noticed how incredibly quiet the boy was when he walked. He kept looking back to make sure he was still there. This surprised the man; young ones were often careless of such things, unaware of the noise they made and how it affected the hunt. Gray Wolf nodded to himself but didn't say anything. The two took their time, setting a leisurely pace. Gray Wolf didn't want to tire the boy, and the boy didn't want to overtax the older man.

They arrived at the pond well before noon, just as the man had planned. The animals would have had their fill of water in the morning, but after hours of grazing, and with the rising heat, they would probably come for a midday drink.

The hunter showed the boy some of the tracks that had been left earlier. There were fresh signs of different animals—a number of deer, and several smaller creatures. There were no bear or wolf tracks. This was good; the presence of wolves, especially, seemed to make the deer and other animals nervous and hunting more difficult. A skittish animal was harder to hit and might cause the man to only wound it; then they would have to track and finish the kill, which could take a long time.

"Boy, I will hide here and will throw my dart when the deer drinks," the hunter instructed. "I plan to wait for the deer to finish drinking first. There is no need to weaken the whole group with thirst. Try to be quiet."

The boy nodded that he understood. To the great surprise of the hunter, and without warning, the boy leapt up very high in the air and grabbed a branch well above Gray Wolf's head. He quickly ascended the tree, seemingly without effort. The tree was in a good spot; the boy would be nearby, but out of the way.

The man didn't show his surprise, but he was inwardly astonished that the boy could climb so high so quickly. The initial leap had been far higher than the man thought the boy would be able to jump, it was more than he would have been able to do—even when he was younger. *This one is certainly full of surprises.*

The two people remained still, quietly breathing, for a long time. The man could feel the sweat trickling down his back as he squatted in the brush. He was happy that he had applied the healer's ointment to keep the biting insects away and only now remembered that he had not done this for the boy. Well, there was nothing he could do now; they must wait without moving. By plan, they were downwind from the pool, but it was impossible to tell from which direction a deer would come. The boy squatted on his branch high above the forest floor. He knew to be quiet, and it was nothing to ignore the small insects and the heat.

They waited for maybe a hand, or perhaps two. Finally, the hunters' patience was rewarded. A small group of deer entered the clearing from the far side of the pond. At first they were hidden. The color of the deer and the seemingly random patterns that formed on their backs and sides are a natural camouflage; it can be difficult to see them in the woods until they move.

First one, then another animal stepped slowly, cautiously up to the pond. They didn't drink right away; deer survive by being careful, alert, and quick. A large doe carefully sampled the smells and the sounds around her before stepping to the water's edge to drink. At least one among the group always kept her head up, watching and listening.

Gray Wolf was patient, waiting for just the right time. He did not want to startle the deer prematurely and wanted them to have their fill of water first. They were mostly does and a few young bucks that were less than one full cycle of seasons. The hunter selected an older doe for his target, one past her birthing seasons.

Once the doe had drunk the water, she backed away from the pond and turned to check the nearby foliage, hoping maybe to find an overlooked delicacy among the plants. Gray Wolf had slowly drawn his arm back with the dart beside his head and was focused on his target. The dart was tipped with a new point, one that he had made with the boy. He did not want the doe to suffer and wanted to kill with a single throw. He concentrated on a spot just behind the shoulder, visualizing the throw in his head, "seeing" how the dart would fly several times first—this had always helped him in the past. He made a small adjustment in aim to compensate for the distance. It was important to be perfect, for both the boy and the deer.

The boy held his breath as he watched the hunter prepare. He saw the strength of the hunter's concentration, and the patience he used to plan his throw. The boy felt sorry for the doe, thinking that she may have been a mother once and would be killed, but at the same time he knew this was an essential part of being a hunter.

Just when the boy was wondering if the man was having second thoughts, the dart leapt from the atlatl and flew to its target as quickly as the boy's eye could follow. It pierced the doe just behind the shoulder and went through her heart, a perfect kill. The deer jumped when she was struck and ran several paces before crashing to the ground. Death was quick, causing only minimal suffering for the doe.

The other deer were startled by the sudden motion and took flight back into the depth of the undergrowth. The two people could hear the rush of their passage through the brush as the sounds faded into the distance.

The man waited a moment before approaching her to make sure that the doe had been killed. Another dart was loaded in his atlatl, but she showed only the normal motions of a fresh kill as the spirit left her body. The thrusting spear was in Gray Wolf's hand as he crossed the space to her anyway. The hunter signed to the boy to join him where the doe lay. Her nerves still made her body quiver, but she would not run again.

Gray Wolf looked at the boy and spoke. "Remember that the deer, like the bison and all of the food taken from the forest and the plains, are a gift. To kill for food and survival is acceptable. Never kill for any other reason and only kill what you need." The boy had heard this before, but it was different this time, being so close and watching it all happen. He would always remember this day.

During the long march back from the bison hunt on the plains the boy had spent much of his time thinking about killing those who shared the forest with him. He'd decided that it was something he had to be willing to do. No hunter rejoiced in the killing of another creature, but it was a part of being a hunter and was done to give life to the people. If he was to be one of them, then he needed to accept this.

Gray Wolf described where he had aimed and why he had chosen this deer and this spot to cast his dart. He was trying to make sure that the boy was a good steward of the land, not just a mindless predator. He explained that it was important not to kill a doe that was pregnant with a fawn, nor to kill one that was still nursing or raising a young one.

"Always do your best to minimize the pain that the animals might feel; if you do not think that you can make a clean kill, do not cast your dart. It is wrong to inflict unnecessary suffering." The boy nodded that he understood; this made it easier for him to accept killing.

"If you do make a mistake and injure the animal, then you must find it and put an end to its suffering—no matter how long it takes." Gray Wolf saw the boy nod again and sighed. He was sure that the boy would eventually be a good hunter, but still worried that the boy couldn't speak. Hunters needed to be able to communicate with one another—signs alone only went so far. But he set his worries aside for now, and the two began field dressing the doe for travel.

Gray Wolf found two small trees for poles that could be used for the journey; they would be strong enough for the load. They tied the legs of the doe to the poles to carry the carcass back to the village using both shoulders. It would be a long trip with such a heavy burden, but worth the effort, since the man wanted the whole deer, not just the meat.

Gray Wolf took the front portion and the boy the rear. Over the next few hours, the two carried their kill back to the village. They didn't arrive until dusk.

The man was pleased with the boy; he lacked the attitude one sometimes saw in other boys and seemed to be very strong for his size, able to keep up even while carrying the heavy burden. Gray Wolf still remembered the leap into the tree. Thinking back, he was sure that he had never seen a person jump that high. The boy certainly was strange, but in a good way.

Several people met them when they arrived and helped prepare the kill for storage. Silver Dawn promised Gray Wolf that she would make a winter wrap for the boy from the hide. It would be the first time anything had been made specifically for him, and the boy looked at the ground to hide how much this little act affected him. People were getting more used to seeing the boy help now. Everyone had watched him train with Gray Wolf, and they were beginning to think of the boy as more than just a permanent stranger.

The hunter nodded his thanks to his brother's mate and clapped the boy on the shoulder. It was a public signal that he thought the boy had done a good job. He would speak with the elders soon, to tell them about the boy's discipline and his ability to learn things quickly. It made Gray Wolf happy to know that he was helping the boy and at the same time adding to the strength of the village.

Dark Sun was watching too. He saw them help the woman skin the animal and then cut fresh meat to share with other members of the village. He never asked himself why the boy's presence should bother him, or why he felt jealousy for a silent outcast orphan with no past and no name. He wanted to know what the boy did in the forest every morning and had already decided to follow him.

Morning Song watched Dark Sun glaring at the boy and felt a shiver. She didn't understand him, but feared what he might be planning to do. She wished she could do something to protect the boy but couldn't think of anything that wouldn't bring trouble for him, and for her. Then she thought about the potential embarrassment. What did it matter if she was embarrassed if she could save him from yet more pain?

7

CONFRONTATION

The boy continued his lessons with Gray Wolf throughout the following days. The older hunter planned to let the boy make his first kill soon, but he wanted to work more on the boy's accuracy from different standing positions first— you never knew from which direction an animal might appear. He also wanted to make sure the boy knew the best places to aim on the different animals, and used an old damaged hide to fashion a surrogate deer for target practice.

His student still spent mornings alone in the forest. Gray Wolf had accepted that this was simply a part of who the boy was, but knew that his charge would obey and be ready when asked.

Five days after the hunt, Dark Sun prepared to follow the boy in the woods again. It would be his third time trying to catch him—the previous times he'd soon lost track of him. The boy seemed to move very fast and the young hunter was not able to find a trace of his passage. It had been frustrating. After all, he was a trained hunter and the boy was just ... well ... a boy. How could he get away so quickly? This time, he anticipated where the boy would go and was waiting not far inside the tree line.

Morning Song had also watched Dark Sun's attempts to follow him and was afraid of what he might do if he caught the boy alone. She had begun to think of the silent boy as a quiet, gentle person who just needed help joining in with the people. She was aware of Dark Sun's temperament and had also heard him complaining about the half animal that others were beginning to like too much. This was the third morning she followed the two into the forest.

It was early; there was just enough light to see where she walked without tripping. The girl knew this might be awkward for her, but refused to stand by while the boy was bullied. Song was determined to intercede on his behalf—especially if it looked like he would be hurt. She was well inside the edge of the forest when she heard an angry voice yelling just ahead.

"I know you've got the old man and a few of the others fooled, but I see you for what you are. Do you hear me?" There was a pause. "Why don't you answer?"

Morning Song walked into a small clearing. Neither of the others had seen her yet. Dark Sun was facing the boy and was leaning towards him, his face distorted in anger. The boy just stood still, looking at the young hunter. He didn't seem alarmed; Song couldn't detect much of a reaction from him at all. However, Dark Sun looked physically tense and was visibly shaking, as though he might be capable of violence. Her fear for the boy made the girl's heart race. She was nervous for herself as well, afraid of being noticed and of what might happen to both the boy and herself. Dark Sun looked almost crazy!

"You're such a strange ... thing. Almost no one wants you here! I saw the way you've been looking at Morning Song. She's the chief elder's granddaughter; you shouldn't even think about her."

Song felt a lump in her stomach hearing this. She hated being used as an excuse for abuse—it horrified her. When she saw Dark Sun's arm come up, as if to grab or push the boy, she knew she had to say something.

"Stop!" she said with a half-strangled voice that didn't sound at all like her own. "What are you doing, Dark Sun? Leave the boy alone!"

The young hunter froze before completing whatever action he had started and looked at her as though she had just struck him. "What is it about him that you all see ... ? You especially!" He turned and reached out with his left arm to push the boy aside, moving towards the girl now. Somehow the boy dodged his hand, but it didn't matter to the young hunter. His focus had shifted to Morning Song, and he crossed to her place by a large tree, still wearing his rage.

"What is it, Morning Song? Are you sorry for him? Do you like him? Did you come here to meet him?" This last part was said more loudly than the rest, and the girl flinched at the venom in his voice—even more than the implication of the question. "He's not one of us. He's half animal. You should spend your time and attention on humans."

The girl opened her mouth to respond, but Dark Sun had grabbed the front of her tunic and was shaking her as he repeated parts of his questions again, not really expecting an answer. Her own anger was rising; she felt a hot flush and made a fist with her free hand. The older boy noticed and could see it in her eyes, although she still hadn't said anything.

"What's the matter with you?" he yelled, pushing her away, and causing her to trip over a root and fall to the ground.

Dark Sun had been almost completely out of control wanting badly to hit someone, but seeing her fall helped to break the madness, and he began to realize what he was doing. He moved towards the girl with his hand out, now thinking to help her up, but saw her eyes widen in fear. She thought Dark Sun was going to hurt her. Just then something heavy struck the young hunter on the back, knocking him forward and causing him to trip over Morning Song's legs and land heavily on another of the tree's exposed roots. The impact momentarily stunned him.

While he was recovering, trying to find his feet, the boy pulled Song from the ground and pointed her back to the village with a gentle push to get her going. The girl hesitated a moment, looking into his eyes, then started to run back towards home to get help. She heard Dark Sun yelling something and was afraid he would catch her—she wasn't sure what he might do. But then the girl heard another heavy thump and guessed that the boy had done something to stop him again. She kept running. The sudden violence, hateful emotions, and fear had brought tears to her eyes, but she didn't sob. She was far too angry for that—and still afraid for the boy.

Back in the clearing, Dark Sun's own fury had drained and his face paled. It was one thing to bully the boy, but he had pushed a defenseless girl of high status down and made her believe that he would harm her. All of the worst things one might expect from an animal. Dark Sun was disgusted with himself and wanted to find the girl to apologize, but the boy was on him again.

He tried to get the boy off his back. The strange mute was horribly strong and managed to evade every attempt by the young hunter to grab him. Once the girl was well gone, he felt himself pushed strongly to the ground again. By the time he could stand, the clearing was empty—no sign of the boy.

Morning Song ran all the way back to her home. When she arrived, the rest of her family was already awake and had seen her coming. Then they saw the tears on her face.

"What happened, Song?" It was Morning Hawk that asked, but her mother and father were suddenly standing behind him, looking at her with frowns on their faces. The girl wasn't sure how to relate what happened, so she told them about how she'd seen Dark Sun watch the boy and what she suspected of his motives. She told them everything quickly and urged them to come with her to help the boy.

"What were you thinking, Song?" Four Bears was angry that she might have been hurt, but this was nothing compared with his fury at Dark Sun. He started moving towards the forest, but Singing Water held his arm and pleaded with him to stop.

"I'll go see that the boy is all right. Hawk and I will get Gray Wolf to check on him. Please don't fight! I don't want to have to heal someone else this morning."

The man looked at his mate, still struggling to control his own anger, and nodded. He understood his mate's concern and knew that he would probably do something he would later regret. Singing Water was the healer, and as the chief elder's only living daughter, her behavior and her family's behavior was scrutinized more than most. But it wasn't easy to do nothing when a man had tried to hurt his daughter; he was secretly thankful for the quick action of the strange, quiet boy. In keeping with the traditions, and to keep the peace, he walked towards the chief elder's home instead of to the forest.

Gray Wolf was appalled when he heard about the altercation between the boy and Dark Sun. The older boy was a hunter now and was expected to behave like a man. He told Hawk to stay in the village, not wanting to make matters worse with too many witnesses, and followed Song to the place where she had last seen the boy. Singing Water followed, carrying her healing basket. She hoped it would not be needed.

They found Dark Sun alone, sitting on the forest floor, his face dark with embarrassment. After the boy had gone, he remained in the clearing thinking and taking a hard look at himself. At some point, a person reaches a place where he's done something outrageous and knows that it's time to look closely at his own behavior. Dark Sun had reached that place. He could no longer make excuses for his temper and was trying to understand what had pushed him to do what he had done. He was even more mortified when he recognized Morning Song and her mother with the older hunter, worried that he might have hurt the girl.

"Where is the boy?" the man asked right away; he was obviously concerned that he had been hurt.

Dark Sun stood, but looked at the ground as he spoke. "He ran away. I didn't harm him."

"What happened?" The man wanted to hear the first thoughts from the older boy, while they were still fresh.

"I followed the boy."

"What was the conflict with the boy about?"

"He did nothing. I don't know what happened inside me, but I was so angry with him ... for nothing."

"Is this the way a hunter, or a man, behaves?"

"No. I was wrong. I should be punished." When he had seen Morning Song fall to the ground, something inside had snapped; he didn't like what he saw in himself.

"Let's not discuss punishment now. That's a matter for the elders. I just want to know what happened and understand that both the boy and the girl will be safe."

"I didn't mean to ..." Dark Sun looked at Morning Song and saw that he had damaged her tunic, and this made him feel even worse. "I'm sorry, Song. I don't know what to say; there is no excuse. Are you okay?"

The girl nodded. She just wanted this to be over.

"I'm sorry," he repeated to everyone.

Back in the village, the elders met with Dark Sun, Gray Wolf, and Morning Song. It was an unusual situation for them. There had been rivalries before, but never between a young hunter and what seemed to be a half-broken child. It didn't make sense to the men, but they could see the depth of Dark Sun's remorse and sensed it might be real.

Later, after they'd had a chance to discuss the matter, they recalled both Gray Wolf, as the boy's temporary guardian, and Dark Sun to council. No one else was permitted to be near. Black Fox spoke for the elders, since Morning Song was the chief elder's granddaughter and it was normal not to mix personal and village matters.

"We believe that you developed this unjustified hatred for the boy and that, perhaps, your feelings towards Morning Song made things worse, but the anger was there before. As a hunter you are expected to follow the traditions even more closely than others, and this time the children were acting more responsibly than you. The girl was simply afraid for the boy's safety and, although she should have brought the matter to our attention, she did nothing wrong in trying to protect him. The boy also thought he was protecting the girl and can be forgiven jumping on your back, and he didn't harm you.

"You are to stay in your home for the next five days, not speaking and only leaving briefly for normal needs. When you have thought on the matter, we want you to return to us to let us know if you still feel as you do now. Afterwards, you will be one of the boy's teachers, under Gray Wolf's guidance, until he is ready to join the hunters. Do you accept?"

Dark Sun nodded, finally looking into the elder's eyes.

"Then go for now. Everything will be forgotten in time, as long as you keep with your commitment."

For Morning Song, the matter wasn't quite over yet. Back at the family lodge, both her mother and her father were upset that she had kept her fears to herself. Morning Hawk just stared at his sister—confusion and disappointment were on his face.

"You might have been hurt," her father said, still angry, but he had accepted the elders' judgment. "What is it about the boy that made you realize what was happening, and why didn't you come for me? Your safety is my responsibility."

"I don't know, Father. I think it's because I don't know if everyone even thinks of the boy as one of us—but I do. He's so alone. I couldn't just do nothing and ignore what I saw. I wasn't being fair to you and mother, but believed that you might not care enough to help him."

Her father shook his head. "Of course we would help the boy; he's more like one of us now than ever before. But even if he was a stranger we would have helped him." Four Bears decided there had been enough said on the subject and stood to leave. He placed his hand on his daughter's shoulder. "I'm very relieved you weren't harmed, Song."

Singing Water looked at her daughter for a while and then smiled at her briefly before starting her own work for the day.

Morning Song hadn't told them everything; she wasn't completely sure herself. She'd imagined she'd heard something, almost like a voice—a whisper really. But it was just one word.

"Run."

8

WHITE FLANK

When enough time had passed and he was sure Morning Song had gotten away safely, the boy leapt directly from the back of Dark Sun into the tree above, quickly scaling its trunk until he was high over the older boy.

It had been a shock to find Dark Sun waiting along the trail, and he was even more surprised by the vehemence the young hunter displayed. Dark Sun was obviously angry about something, but the boy didn't know what had caused this sudden and rather extreme response, until he saw Morning Song. Before she arrived, he had thought it better to let the older boy exhaust his anger. The things Dark Sun said were disturbing; other people had said similar things, but not quite so bluntly. It made him wonder if more people felt the same way, and if he was fooling himself that he could be one of them.

Living as he had among different families, watching others when they forgot he was there, had given him unusual insight into how people behaved. The boy had stayed in almost every home at one time or another and, eventually, most people didn't care what he heard. Why be concerned over the thoughts of a poor, broken mute boy? He had often heard people say things when they were angry that they didn't mean. Most of the time people forgave and forgot quickly. When they didn't, friction in a home could last a long time; in the end the result was usually the same—people just lost time being angry if they allowed things to persist. Angry rants sometimes did more harm to the person yelling than to those at whom it was directed. It was a pattern he had seen repeated in certain families, especially during the deepest part of winter, and during the storms, when everyone was confined inside. The boy wanted to let Dark Sun's own storm pass quickly. The appearance of the girl had changed things.

He knew right away that Morning Song had come out of worry for him. It was a thing he hadn't expected from anyone, except maybe Gray Wolf. The fact that the girl would even consider deflecting some of Dark Sun's anger towards herself had brought a strange, warm feeling around the boy's heart. But what Dark Sun had said about Morning Song was right. He *had* noticed her lately. There was something calming about her presence—but she was the chief's granddaughter.

When it looked as though the older boy might harm the girl in his rage, the boy had sprung into action. He would not allow Dark Sun to hurt her, and threw himself onto the back of the young hunter before he could hit Song. When the older boy tripped, there was just enough time to help the girl up.

The boy reached down and pulled Morning Song from the ground and then urged her to run home, even pointing out the right direction, in case she had lost track when she fell. When he spoke to her in his silent language, urging her on, he almost imagined that his thoughts had been loud enough to hear. Then he leapt onto Dark Sun's back again to allow the girl time. He needed to know that she was safe, but didn't want to hurt the older boy either. It was easy to evade the young hunter's attempts to grapple him; he was so much slower than the boy. Once he was sure the girl was safely away, he left.

After ascending the tree, the boy used branches of the middle canopy to get clear of the area before dropping down to run. He needed to think about what had happened and what to do. The boy always did his best thinking as he ran.

He was disturbed by the words, more than the ranting of the older boy. People had said such things about him before—was this how they truly felt? But, the girl's presence had disturbed him even more...disturbed wasn't the right word. Affected. Yes, the girl's action had affected him. It said that he was worthy of her friendship; he was something more than just another...thing. He remembered now the way she had looked at him when he returned from the bison hunt—a welcoming look, even relief, as if she had been worried about him. The two messages, Dark Sun's and Morning Song's, conflicted with each other.

He was following one of the deer trails, absent-mindedly watching for signs as he thought about everything, when a familiar pattern caught his eye. His brain processed it before he realized what was familiar, and he stopped to examine it more closely. These were the tracks of a deer, but not just any deer—he had seen these before. The rear hoof imprints fell inside of the broad front footfalls; certainly it was a large buck with a very broad chest. One rear foot consistently carried just a bit less weight than the other and was slightly misaligned, as if the left leg had been injured at some time in the past, and had healed imperfectly. The boy thought back to the day he'd watched Red Sky teaching the other boys about tracking a particular deer. The pattern matched the tracks that Red Sky had described and shown the boys. These were the tracks of White Flank, the boy was sure of it.

He thought about what to do. He hadn't brought his weapon and, in any event, wasn't sure that he wanted to hunt White Flank. Also, Gray Wolf had not told him that he could hunt yet, and the boy didn't want to disappoint the man. He decided that he would track the buck, but just for practice. This was a good opportunity to improve his skill and to test himself. The boy was curious to know how fast he could move while still tracking a particular animal in a real exercise.

The sharpness of the imprints at their edges told him that the deer had passed very recently, sometime this morning. He knew Red Sky could have narrowed the time down more accurately, but this was good enough for his own game. He began following the tracks, looking for other signs along the way. He could move along while tracking, but not really what he would call fast—not if he didn't want to lose the deer's trail. As he worked, the boy began to see other signs that stood out, things he hadn't noticed before, subtle indications that a large buck had passed recently. Sometimes it was just a small, freshly broken branch hanging from a tree; sometimes it was a fragment of hair captured in a burr or wedged in the bark of a tree. The boy was getting used to spotting these kinds of things, and he decided to move a little faster.

As the day passed, he was putting the little pieces of information together in his mind more quickly— the tracks, the disturbed brush, the occasional lost hair, as well as other things, all of which gave him a fresh perspective and a new appreciation for this skill. As he gained insight, he began to imagine that he could almost see the deer running ahead of him and tried to predict where the deer would run next, testing his predictions as he ran. He envisioned where White Flank would choose to shift towards a different path to make better progress north, and then saw that the deer had done precisely that. This was fun! The longer he focused, the more "open" his vision became, and the faster he could move. His speed increased gradually without losing the signs, until ... yes! There was the buck, ahead of him now!

White Flank was foraging, moving slowly now and working his way towards a spring where he could drink. The buck sensed a presence, but when he stood still and listened very hard he didn't hear anything. There was no taste of threat in the air, no sound of a stalker. Still, the buck was uneasy but returned to eating the last shoots of the season. Before long it would be winter and easy food would be scarce.

The boy sensed something about the deer's presence too, something he couldn't quite describe, a vague sense of familiarity, even kinship—but he didn't know why. Deer were food for him now, not family, and the boy frowned at this strange feeling. It was at this moment that White Flank heard something coming through the forest from the opposite direction and turned quickly to run back towards the boy. He was startled to find the boy so close but rapidly changed direction and avoided hitting the young human.

The boy decided he would run with White Flank, to see who was faster. He couldn't yet hear what had startled the buck. The deer had four legs and they were long, but the forest was very dense here and the buck couldn't run far in a straight line; he was never able to reach full speed. The boy had an advantage there; he was nimble, quick, and small. He could slide by the bush that White Flank needed to jump over or plow through, and the boy's speed didn't vary much as he dashed left and right or ducked to avoid obstacles. It seemed almost an even match for now. Before long, even the boy could hear something coming from behind them. He glanced quickly over his shoulder and felt a cold chill as the sounds reached him. There were three wolves chasing them, and they had begun to growl in their own wolf hunting language. The wolves were gaining ground—and they were very fast.

The three predators ran along parallel paths—one was directly behind the prey and the two others were running to the left and right to contain them in case they changed direction. The boy knew that he was fast, but not as fast as a wolf. White Flank might have been able to get away if the undergrowth were less dense and he was able to run in a straight line, but the densely packed branches, shrubs, and other vegetation were impeding his progress. Even if he could gain some distance, the wolves were endurance runners and would probably get him eventually.

The boy wished that he had brought some kind of weapon, an atlatl or a spear, but all he had was his small flint knife, used for eating and cleaning game. Its blade was short and set in a handle made from an antler. It was not a hunting weapon, but its flint blade was razor sharp. The boy knew that he could escape—not by running, but he could leap into a tall tree if necessary—but something was stopping him. For some reason, he wasn't ready to abandon White Flank to the wolves. It seemed insane, but if he could stay on the ground for now, maybe he could draw them away.

The buck was terrified and struggling to run through the brush. Panic was reducing his efficiency and made his progress even slower. They were both losing the race with the wolves.

The boy knew the wolves could outrun him in a straight line and that they were quick in the forest too, but he remained calm, thinking about what to do. He deliberately began veering around obstacles left and right to put them in the path of the closest wolf, gaining a little time. There was always the tree.... The boy was thinking hard and remembered the fight between the wolverine and the two wolves. The wolverine was quick and agile, always turning to attack the wolves' flanks with its sharp claws before dancing away from the wolves' teeth. The boy thought he might be able to do something like this too. Well, maybe with one wolf but not two or three. He was not a wolverine.

He could hear the thumping of feet from a wolf now, striking the forest floor close behind. It was a regular rapid beat and sounded more like the hooves of a bison on the plains than a wolf in the forest. Soon he began to hear the wolf's breath, panting in rhythm with its stride. It was getting closer, and was already too close. One way or another, the boy knew he would have to do something very soon.

There were just a few dozen heartbeats left to decide when an idea came to him, but he needed something more to make his idea work. He saw his opportunity and veered sharply left— impossibly, speeding up just a whisker more. He wanted to pass very close to a small tree, one with a clear enough space under its branches. The wolf nearest to him turned to follow, just on his heels. The boy was running faster than he had ever run in his life, and he could hear the wind passing over his body. The wolf's fangs were just behind him now and he could almost feel its hot breath when he reached the tree at breathtaking speed.

As he passed, the boy reached out with his left arm and used the trunk to pull his body into a tight circle around the tree with unimaginable quickness. The force on his arm was terrible, but he held on and kept the knife in his right hand, its blade down and its edge outwards, away from his arm. The quick rotation around the tree put him just behind the wolf and he slashed at its hindquarters, sharply and with purpose, putting his entire being into the strike.

The boy felt the blade slide across and into one of the wolf's hind legs, exactly where the main tendon was. Something seemed to snap above the wolf's knee and he let go of the tree to run away at an angle from the wolf's path of travel—before it could turn to bite him. He heard the wolf's surprise in its cry of pain as it stopped running. One of its hind legs was useless, but it wasn't ready to give up fighting yet. Even with three legs, he should be able to kill a human puppy! Normally he would have been right, but maybe not this particular puppy.

The boy began circling the wolf, using trees and other objects to change direction rapidly. He'd use his hand or put a foot on the side of a tree, tilting steeply and running with his body almost parallel to the ground in a sharp curve, all to confuse the wolf. It seemed not to matter to him where the ground was as he circled the wolf for the third time.

The wolf was confounded by the young boy's speed and quickness. As he spun around, he began to wonder, who was the predator and who was the prey? The wolf turned repeatedly, slowed by its useless leg, lunging as the boy came close but missing when his prey pulled away from his teeth just in time. The wolf was trying to understand from which direction the boy would attack next when he lost track of the silent runner, just for a moment—but it was an important moment.

The boy saw his chance and dashed at the wolf from behind. He slashed the wolf's other hind leg with his knife before leaping up to grab a branch to avoid the wolf's fangs. He almost made it unscathed, but the wolf managed to briefly sink its teeth into his leg and tear a fleshy part from his calf. The boy felt the pain and sensed the warm flow of blood but ignored it for now. The teeth had not torn into muscle and the wound wouldn't affect his ability to climb or run.

The nearest wolf had heard the cry of its pack mate when its leg had been cut and was approaching the tree now. Its brother lay writhing in pain on the ground, no longer able to walk but dragging its body with just its front paws. The second wolf could see the boy in the tree but couldn't reach him. Frustrated, he snarled at the human—if only he could leap high enough to get him! Just then another cry rang through the forest.

White Flank understood that he could not outrun the wolves and had decided to fight too. One lone wolf was still chasing him and had expected to hear its brothers' voices beside him on the hunt, but something had diverted them—maybe the human. Now he was alone and the strong buck was facing him with its large, impressive antlers. He paused and the hesitation gave White Flank the opening and encouragement he needed. The wolf's confusion turned to surprise and pain when White Flank lifted the wolf in his antlers, goring him and throwing him backwards. One of the wolf's front legs and several of its ribs were broken. The wolf couldn't breathe without intense pain and was no longer interested in fighting.

Hearing his cry, the last unscathed wolf took off towards the sound of the fight with the buck. After all, the deer was food and the human puppy was not important. The boy watched the wolf take off to the southwest, leaving its injured pack mate at the base of the tree. The wounded wolf was also distracted by the sound of battle and didn't sense the boy drop down until he was on the wolf's back ... too late.

The boy had reversed the knife in his hand and, reaching from above, slashed its throat before leaping free. The animal thrashed around briefly, but soon the loss of blood took its toll and he was still.

The boy was elated, relieved, and shaking from the adrenaline that still ran through his veins, but he knew that he wasn't done yet. Maybe it was just the bloodlust of battle or maybe it was something else driving him—the boy ran after the last wolf.

He was moving like the wind rushing across the plains. His newfound confidence pushed him to a speed he didn't know he was capable of achieving.

The boy had forgotten his wound, forgotten his fear, and forgotten everything else completely. He was a wild creature now, determined that the wolf would not kill White Flank. There was no rational reason for him to help the buck, but rationality had vanished, and been replaced with something else—the burning purpose had been ignited again, somewhere deep inside. It was the same burning purpose that drove him to run in the forest, which demanded perfection in everything he did, and the same compelling drive that had fueled his run for days following the massacre of his village. There were no half measures with the boy and few things, short of death, that could stop him.

He caught up with the wolf as it was attacking the buck, trying to take White Flank down by a hind leg—and succeeding. The boy blazed by the wolf, slashing one of its hind legs, just as he had done with its brother. He struck so hard that the predator's leg was partially severed.

The wolf was in shock and let go of the deer, spinning on his three remaining legs to defend himself from this ferocious new enemy. But the boy had already thrown his body into a new direction and was circling again, looking for the animal to make a mistake. The wolf spun around again, trying to decide where to attack the boy. He was confused and angry, but he had forgotten about the strong buck. White Flank rammed into the wolf's side, throwing him in the air, and then brought his hooves down onto the wolf's back. The boy heard the wolf yelp in pain, saw that both wolves nearby were severely injured, and knew that the fight was over. There was one more responsibility.

Looking around, he found a heavy tree branch nearby; it was narrow on one end and thick on the other, shaped like a club. He stood outside the range of the wolves' fangs and used the club to finish them, ending their agony. The boy noticed a strange noise as he killed them; it sounded like the roar of a savage animal fighting, but its source was a complete mystery until he realized that it was coming from his own mouth. Finally, it was all finished.

Still shaking, he fell to his knees, spent. The boy wasn't sure how much time passed, but eventually realized where he was again and found that he was able to stand. His legs were still shaking from their exertion and the sudden loss of adrenaline. He was stunned to find that White Flank was still there!

The deer should have run away to safety. It didn't look as though it was seriously injured, and the boy wondered briefly if the buck now thought of him as a threat. He considered dashing to the nearest tree to leap into the safety of its outstretched arms, but the buck hadn't taken a threatening stance. The two stared at each other for a while in silence; only the sound of their heavy breathing could be heard in the quiet. Neither knew exactly what to make of the other, but each had a sense of recognition.

For the buck, the boy's scent had spurred a memory from long, long ago, when he was just a fawn. He remembered coming upon a strange human fawn sleeping on the floor of his forest. The buck's mother had allowed him to approach the human to learn its scent and to understand its shape. He could still remember that scent. This was the same human, somewhat larger than before, but the same. After a few moments, the buck raised its head, almost a nod, then turned to disappear into the trees. The boy fell back to his knees for a while to rest again.

He wanted to take the hides as gifts and so used his knife to deftly skin the two wolves in the clearing. Then he went back to the first wolf's body to skin that as well. The three hides were all that he could carry; the meat of predators was not considered food. The boy found a stream on the way home and took time to wash in its water. His wound looked worse than it felt, but it did sting. He knew that it was time to get back to the village.

Gray Wolf had been waiting for the boy since the affair with Dark Sun and wasn't sure what he might be thinking. The man was trying to fashion new points, but had already broken one promising stone due to carelessness. The boy liked to spend time in the forest and Gray Wolf was worried that the conflict might have driven him away for a longer time than normal. He had expected the boy to return earlier. It was time to speak with him about his first hunt, time that the boy took on more responsibility—for the good of the people. Unable to speak, the boy could never be a leader and would always be a lower-ranked hunter, but as a hunter he would be cherished. Gray Wolf was also determined to continue teaching the boy how to make weapons. This skill would add to his status in the village. It was very late now—the boy usually returned by noon. Could something have happened to him, or was his lateness due to the incident this morning?

While he was thinking about everything, Morning Song came to where he was working and sat across from him. The older man looked at her expectantly. When she didn't say anything he returned to making stone points. The girl seemed to have a calming influence on him and the weapon maker's work improved. The two accepted each other's presence in silence.

Morning Song stayed with him until the sun passed towards the western horizon.

"I should help my mother," Song said at last, getting up to leave.

The hunter nodded, smiling slightly at the girl.

The sun was less than two hands from the horizon when Gray Wolf decided to approach the elders to ask for help finding the boy. After the events of the morning, he was sure they would be receptive. While walking to the center of the village, he saw a strange creature come out of the forest. It looked half human and half animal, but he recognized the boy's form under the hides. The shape was large and covered with fur and blood, but was still the boy. Gray Wolf sighed deeply.

The boy was carrying fur hides, more than one; they looked like fresh wolf skins. Others in the village had seen the strange figure emerge from the forest as well. At first people were startled by the strange apparition; one or two hunters jumped up to get their weapons, but they stopped when they realized it was just the strange boy carrying furs. Where did he get them? Everyone wondered the same thing. Did he steal them? Whose traps had he robbed?

Gray Wolf walked to the boy to help with his burden. They headed for the village center, the heart of the village, where the elders met. The boy's exhaustion was visible in his over-bright eyes. He had an injury that the healer would tend soon, but Gray Wolf knew that people would need an explanation. There was a lot of blood on the boy but most of it was not his. The hunter noted the composure and self-confidence that he displayed; something important had happened today. He bent to examine the injury on the boy's leg, but it didn't look serious and could wait a short while.

The people were collecting at the central fire to learn what had happened. They wanted to know where the strange boy had found the wolf hides. The three elders gathered together to listen and to ask questions. Many of the hunters were curious too and stepped closer to listen.

The man and the boy laid the three pelts on the ground. The hunters could see the injuries to the wolves on the hides. They didn't understand the hind-leg injuries and thought these might have been damage caused during the skinning process.

Gray Wolf pointed to the three hides and asked, "Where did you find these?"

The boy misunderstood and thought he was asking where he had found the wolves. He pointed to the forest and made an arching sign, indicating a great distance. He didn't speak, of course.

"Were the wolves dead in a trap? Whose wolves are these?"

"Is this how the boy hunts?" someone asked. "Does he just take what he wants from other hunters?" There was a general shaking of heads by many who thought this must be the case. They were thinking that maybe Dark Sun had been right about the boy. Morning Song had come and was watching without an expression; she didn't believe that he would steal—his defense of her that morning had strengthened her confidence in him.

"Maybe it's a bad idea to train the boy. There is no telling what he might do," another person added.

The boy was confused and shook his head, pointing to himself to indicate that the wolves were his. The people around the fire laughed, but one of the village elders held up his hand, demanding silence.

Gray Wolf smiled to himself, but shook his head. It was clear the boy simply didn't understand all of the rules between people. They would need to find whoever had placed the traps and bring the furs to them and apologize. The People didn't want trouble with another village. There was at least one within several days' travel, and Gray Wolf knew he might have to go there. He would take the boy with him as a lesson.

Gray Wolf thought that a few of the people were rushing to judgment. He would ask to speak at the next village council. Just like Dark Sun, people sometimes formed hasty opinions, but the people of the village were fair. First, they needed to find out exactly what had happened.

"I know that you brought them, but the real question is who trapped them, who killed them?" Gray Wolf understood that the boy was simply trying to help the village, and he knew that the elders understood this too. That's why they were elders. Then the boy shocked the entire village—even Gray Wolf and Morning Song were surprised.

"We killed," the boy said. "White Flank and me killed wolves." If it wasn't grammatically correct, the boy could be excused. After all, he hadn't spoken in many years, not since before he came to live here.

The people were talking again, all at once and in amazement. No one knew that the boy could speak. Morning Song's best friend, Squirrel, looked at her with widened eyes.

"Did you know?" she mouthed. Song shook her head in equal amazement, and relief. She felt, somehow, that her opinion of him had been vindicated.

"You can speak?" Gray Wolf asked incredulously.

The boy smiled and nodded. "I can speak, not good, but I can speak."

The chief elder, Great Storm, held up his hand for quiet. The boy looked directly into the old man's face for the first time. His skin was like leather and he had sharp, angular features that had weathered through the years, but his back was straight, and a pair of ageless black eyes peered back at the boy, evaluating him as a person.

"Tell me, boy, how did you kill these three wolves, and who is this White Flank who helped you?"

Still looking at the elder, the boy nodded that he understood the question. This was the first time in his life that he could remember the village chief speaking directly to him, and of course it was in front of the whole village.

"I track... tracked White Flank. White Flank is buck, but now like brother in some way." This made the village elder frown—something didn't make sense here.

"You say that this White Flank is a deer, a buck, and that you were tracking him. Were you hunting White Flank?"

"No. I only track. Before, I watch Red Sky track White Flank. He say different buck have different sign." And the boy drew the tracks of White Flank in the dirt, showing the size of the buck as well as the slightly misaligned left leg. Red Sky was in the group watching and he frowned. He walked to where the boy drew the tracks and nodded.

"Yes, I tracked a buck with these signs. I was showing Dark Sun and Morning Hawk how one could track a particular buck." He looked at the boy. "But I didn't see you."

"I was with White Flank when you and others come," the boy said. "I hide and follow to learn how to track, watching lesson." Red Sun was stunned... and flattered that his lesson had been so well absorbed, even if he had been unaware of the student.

"So," the village elder continued. "You were tracking this buck and found the wolves trapped?"

The boy shook his head and took a deep breath to slow down.

"I track White Flank to see how fast can I run and track at same time. I track for long time and find White Flank many hands' walk." And the boy pointed in the direction from which he had come. The elders understood what he meant.

"I think it take long time to find him, only I run while I track and find him fast, maybe more than one hand...less than two." The boy didn't know how to explain that he could run fast, faster than the fastest hunter, and he wasn't sure that he wanted to discuss this in front of everyone.

"Okay," Great Storm said. "You found this buck, after tracking him for between one and two hands, and then what happened?"

"I watch White Flank and then three wolves come. Wolves chase White Flank and me through forest. We run very fast but not fast as wolves." People in the crowd began muttering to each other.

The elder was frowning too; this was unexpected. He had thought the boy would just say that he found the wolves trapped and finished them off somehow; now it seemed the boy was claiming that the wolves pursued him and this buck he called White Flank.

"Go on with your story," Great Storm prodded.

"We run different direction. White flank go right, I go left." And the boy showed with his hands how they had diverged at different angles. "One wolf follow me and two follow White Flank. I am fast, but not fast as wolf. Then I remember time I see wolverine fight two wolves and I think I fight my wolf same way." The boy could hear the comments of the people around him get louder, but he went on anyway.

Morning Song was following the story with everyone else, but noticed now that the boy had an injury on his leg. Like her mother, she was drawn to healing, and the wound distracted her from some of the story.

"Fight how? What weapon did you have?" Gray Wolf interjected as he signaled his apology to the elders for his interruption.

"I have knife," the boy said, holding up his flint blade.

This drew even more reaction from the people. "How can a boy fight a wolf with just a small knife?" This was Laughing Bear, disbelief heavy in his voice.

Once again the chief elder signaled for patience and requested that the people follow the traditions. "I am speaking with the boy now. Everyone will have their chance to say what they want."

Laughing Bear nodded his apology, embarrassment clear on his face.

"Please go on with your story, boy," Great Sky requested calmly.

"I run fast, faster than ever run before, but still wolf getting closer."

The chief nodded at this; obviously the boy couldn't outrun a wolf.

"I hold knife like this." The boy showed how he had held the knife during the fight. "I run to tree with wolf very close, can feel breath. I do this with tree." And the boy mimicked whirling around the tree using his left arm. "Go behind wolf and I cut his leg, here." And the boy made the slashing motion with his knife and pointed to the hind leg on one of the wolves.

Great Storm had been watching the boy as he spoke, looking for the signs of a lie. It was difficult to fool him. He was surprised that he saw no sign of one, but then the boy had never talked before. This was certainly turning out to be an entertaining story and an interesting afternoon! It would be even more interesting if it were true.

"You cut his leg, so he couldn't chase you, but he was still able to fight. Did you run?"

The boy shook his head no. "I want kill wolf then, am angry."

The people could see something in his eyes form, a kind of affront at the wolf's audacity in wanting to hunt him. There was a murmur as people commented both on what he said and how he said it.

"Then I run circles," the boy continued, "always twisting direction."

Yes, that is certainly how a wolverine fights, the elder thought.

"I cut other leg and jump over wolf for tree. I climb tree but still wolf bite leg, not bad." The boy showed his leg to the people and, yes, there was clearly an injury.

Gray Wolf had earlier seen the sign of the teeth in the boy's flesh. The elders were more alert now, the physical evidence was starting to add up, but still it was hard to believe that a slow boy who had never been taught to hunt could be such a fierce fighter. They could see the wolf sign on the boy's leg now and nodded for him to continue.

"Other wolf come for me, he hear my wolf scream. I wait in tree so other wolf not get me. Then we all hear wolf with White Flank scream."

The elders frowned at this. Yes, occasionally a lone wolf could fall victim to a strong buck, but it was rare.

"Other wolf run to help. Then I jump down on my wolf from tree and kill." The boy made the motion of cutting the wolf's throat and, again, showed the result on one of the wolf hides.

The people were looking at the boy differently now—was there a new sense of respect? They were beginning to think that some of what he said might be true. They were also enthralled with his story and glad when the elder urged him to go on. The boy was growing anxious with so many people being there and kept looking around at all of the faces. This was the first time he had spoken. Until now he had been mostly focused on the elders and Gray Wolf, but he realized that he was speaking with the whole village present. While looking around he locked eyes with Morning Song for a moment and she smiled at him encouragingly. The elder closest to him put a hand on his arm sympathetically and nodded for him to continue.

"I chase other wolf."

The people frowned and shook their heads at this, why would a boy chase a second wolf after narrowly escaping one?

"I know White Flank fight one wolf, but maybe other wolf would get him so I run very, very fast. I find wolf. He has leg of White Flank in teeth and I run fast and cut back leg, very hard." And he showed his slashing motion again and then showed the almost-detached leg on the last wolf's pelt.

Gray Wolf could see the elder's mouth was open now. No one had ever heard of a boy hunting wolves with only a small knife in his hands and then see that boy come into the village with three fresh wolf hides. Even if it were not true, this would be a story told around the fire for a long time.

"Wolf turn and want to fight me. I start circling like wolverine again. Then White Flank attack wolf and hurt him, two wolves hurt very bad. I find big stick and kill wolves. I hit head of wolves many times." He didn't describe the strange exchange with the buck—not only did he consider it too personal, but he was also not sure exactly what had happened. "Later, White Flank leave. I take skin from wolves and bring gift for friends." Here the boy looked at the older hunter and saw a strange expression on the man's face. Was he sad? No, Gray Wolf smiled at him.

Telling what had happened now, even the boy understood how hard the story would be to accept. He could hardly believe his luck today and was thankful that both he and the buck had survived.

But, he was exhausted and his leg was starting to hurt more; the events of the day were catching up with him. The elders saw this too; they saw his fatigue and pain and understood how it felt when such a day finally ended. Kindly, they asked Singing Water to help the boy and requested that everyone hold their questions for later, after he'd had time to rest.

"Rest now, boy. Please excuse our rudeness for not making you comfortable first. We were very surprised. Later we would like to speak with you again." Someone, the boy thought it was Wild Flower, Red Sky's mate, took the wolf hides. If the story were true these three hides would become a powerful talisman for the boy and for the village. She wanted to get help working the furs.

The people were already talking about the story as the boy was led to Gray Wolf's lodge, where his wound was treated and he was allowed to sleep.

Singing Water cleaned the wound, noting the clear signs of canine teeth in his flesh. She applied a poultice that would stay for the night to draw out the poison that might cause an infection, and then she wrapped his calf with a clean protective rabbit-skin bandage. Morning Song had wanted to help, but the healer didn't allow the girl to accompany her. Singing Water had seen the bewildering attachment her daughter had for the boy but hadn't made up her mind about him; she needed more time to think. After treating the boy, she leaned over and placed her hand on his shoulder.

"Rest tonight, and only walk when absolutely necessary until I look at the leg again tomorrow." She paused a moment, wanting to say more. "Thank you for protecting Song today. I hope you know that Dark Sun's words were not a sign of how the village feels towards you." The boy closed his eyes briefly and nodded once. Singing Water took his hand and squeezed it before leaving. She had never noticed before how much presence there was in his eyes and wondered how many times in the past she too had been unfair to him.

After the boy had gone to rest and people had returned to their own activities, the elders asked both Gray Wolf and Red Sky to join them for a discussion. People stayed away from the immediate area, knowing that the elders wanted privacy.

The men sat in a circle, each lost in thought for a while.

"Well," Great Storm said at last. "What are your thoughts?"

Black Fox was the first to speak. "The story was a good one. If true, the boy would be an amazing hunter. How do we know what's true? One thing is for sure, we have been wrong about the boy for years. Why hasn't he spoken before today?"

"Those are good questions, especially the last one. I think it is important that we find the truth about his story." Great Storm gave no sign of whether he believed or didn't believe it all. "The physical evidence seems to support him, but we see only pieces. Gray Wolf, you have spent the most time with the boy—what have you seen in him? Could his story be true? Or, is he the kind of boy who might make up such a thing?"

Gray Wolf hesitated for a moment, wanting to be objective. "I've worked with the boy for some time now and have found him to be a quick learner and a hard worker. I've seen none of the things I might expect of a person who creates lies. We all know that the boy spends a lot of time in the forest. I suspect that we still don't really know him as well as we think.

"The boy has surprised me several times," Gray Wolf continued. "The first was when he showed up at the hunt, uninvited and undetected, days from here and ready to work. On the journey, he seemed much brighter than I would have expected, useful. Later, as I taught him something about making weapons, he did exceptional work and learned fast.

"When we hunted the doe, there were other things I noticed but set aside at the time as part of my imagination. The boy moves very well in the forest. He never seems to make a sound, and when we were setting up for the trap at the water pool, I saw him leap into a tree and climb as if he had been born in its branches. I had half forgotten this, but he surprised me with that leap—it was like a deer jumping. I don't think I've ever seen a person jump that high, and he's still just a boy."

Everyone nodded at the hunter's words.

"What about you, Red Sky?"

"He remembered the tracking lesson perfectly. If he's gained so much knowledge that he could track on the run, just by listening from a distance—if that's true—then he is the best student I've had and might become a great tracker. I was impressed with his memory, and I hope his story is true. Like Black Fox, I can't understand how we missed such a boy who has lived here for years. I feel ashamed not to have noticed him."

The elders all nodded in agreement at this; each felt a share of the blame for how the boy had been neglected. The village couldn't afford to throw away such talent. The five men sat for a while thinking in silence, until Gray Wolf made a suggestion.

"We could check the story. There must be other physical evidence where the fight occurred. Let me take the boy to find the truth. I suggest that you choose another hunter to come with me."

Great Storm had been waiting for someone to suggest this. "I agree with your plan, Gray Wolf. Now, please check on the boy. Red Sky, would you stay a moment?"

Gray Wolf nodded and left to check on the boy. After he had gone, Great Storm spoke with Red Sky. "I think that you are best equipped to examine the signs and check the truth of the story. Will you accompany Gray Wolf?"

"Of course. It will be interesting to see how well he can track too."

"Come back when you have learned the truth." Great Storm was satisfied that they had a plan.

9

THE NAMING

The next morning, the boy woke well after the sun was above the hill. His leg still hurt, but not badly, and he had no difficulty getting up and walking around. After a while it felt less stiff and he ignored it. The other people in the village looked at him strangely today. He had gone from being invisible to being all too visible. It made him want to run into the forest, but he fought the urge, knowing instinctively that now was not the time to be isolated.

Gray Wolf was waiting for him with breakfast and an herbal tea provided by the healer. Singing Water asked to look at his leg again and had brought Morning Song with her today. Singing Water unwrapped and examined the leg. The bleeding had finally stopped seeping and the wound looked clean. She nodded to herself and told the boy that his leg was doing well.

"Is his leg well enough to travel?" Gray Wolf wanted to know.

"He should be fine, but keep the wrap on to protect it."

The adults left Song and the boy alone for a few moments. She had pleaded with her mother to let her come, saying she wanted to thank him for stopping Dark Sun.

Morning Song finally looked up into the boy's eyes. "Thank you," they both said in unison, and then laughed at themselves.

"I hope you not hurt yesterday," the boy said.

"No. I was fine, just surprised."

"Thing okay with Dark Sun?"

"Yes, he'll be fine. I think he's even more embarrassed than I was."

"You help me. No need for embarrass... to be embarrassed. Sorry not talk good." The boy was not used to actually making his sentences, but he understood and could hear his own mistakes.

"You speak well enough; with practice you'll be perfect. You can always practice with me." Song looked back at the floor of the shelter for a moment before continuing. "May I ask you something? It's been bothering me for many days."

He smiled with encouragement.

"I thought I saw you in the trees the day that Red Sky took the boys into the forest to practice tracking. Was that you?"

The boy's eyes opened wider and he smiled, thinking about how clever he thought he had been that day. "Yes, I saw you near river, did not know you saw me."

"How do you fly through the trees like that?"

"Practice. If like, you can always practice with me."

"I think I'll stay on the ground for now," the girl replied, laughing. "I'll see you later," the girl offered.

"I'll see you later," the boy said, copying her again, and smiling as the girl left.

The boy walked outside, just as Singing Water was turning to leave. "Don't worry," she said to Gray Wolf and looked at the boy. "The leg will heal well."

The hunter wanted to ask him something but seemed hesitant and did not look directly at him at first. The boy wondered why, but pretended not to notice the old man's unease. Finally, Gray Wolf broke the silence.

"Boy, can you take me to the place where you fought the wolves? Would you be able to find it again?" He could still hardly believe the relief he'd felt when he learned that the boy could speak.

"Yes, I can take," the boy answered.

"How does your leg feel?" the older man wanted to know, concern was in his voice.

"Leg fine ... is fine—we leave soon?"

Gray Wolf nodded.

As the two prepared to enter the forest, Red Sky approached them.

"Gray Wolf, do you mind if I come with you and the boy?"

The older man looked at the boy, thinking for a moment and allowing time for him to react, even if it wasn't his decision. "No, Red Sky, I do not mind; you are welcome to join us." He was happy with whom the elders had chosen.

Red Sky was curious about the fight, but even more curious about the boy's tracking skills. He wanted to assess these for himself. He would ask the boy to follow White Flank's trail again and to point out the signs as he saw them.

"Boy," he asked, "can you show me where you first saw White Flank's tracks and then how you were guided to the buck?"

The boy nodded solemnly.

The first part of their journey was made in silence. The boy knew that the two hunters were watching him closely, but he trusted both of these men. He respected Red Sky's skill and appreciated the patience he had shown with the other boys. After traveling at a leisurely pace, they arrived at the place where he had first seen White Flank's tracks.

"Here are tracks of White Flank," the boy announced.

Red Sky bent over the tracks and examined them closely. "Yes, they are from the same buck that I saw before. Your eyes are sharp," he added. "Now, can you show us how fast you can follow? I know that some of the signs have faded, so it would be understandable if you needed to move more slowly." He looked up at the boy from his kneeling position, wanting to see how confident he was in his skill. To his surprise, the boy smiled.

"I can follow, easy." Clearly he had no doubt that he could follow the path that he had taken yesterday.

"Can you show me how fast you can track?" Another test.

The boy laughed aloud. It was the first time either man could remember ever hearing the boy make that sound, but he nodded, smiling.

"Ready?" the boy asked.

"Let's go," the two men said together.

The boy dashed forward, following a trail, moving at what he considered an easy pace, not real running. Even so, it was all the men could do to keep up with him. As the boy ran he kept pointing out signs for Red Sky. The hunter was sure that even he might have missed one or two of the little pieces of information at this speed, but he could see that the boy was visualizing how the deer moved, just as he would do. Eventually they reached the place where the boy said he had watched the buck.

"That was very fast," Red Sky said, panting. Gray Wolf was out of breath too and a little behind, but he could tell that the tracker had met his match. The boy, still breathing easily, didn't seem tired at all.

"This is where I watch White Flank. There, you see his tracks when he almost hit me."

Red Sky saw the place where the deer must have dodged the boy when he ran away from the wolves. And then he found the wolf tracks too—there were three of them.

The men followed as he led them slowly to where his first wolf kill had happened. The boy had noticed that Gray Wolf was moving more slowly and reminded himself that the man was not young.

Finally they arrived at the scene of the battle. The carcass of the first wolf was still there, still under the tree where the boy had stopped. They could see where the leg tendons had been cut and noted the deep slice through the throat. Next, the boy took the men to the place where the other two wolves were killed.

The hunters examined the wounds of the other wolves and spoke quietly with each other. It was clear that they were impressed, but they were still absorbing evidence, and were careful not to say anything. The elders had instructed them to investigate, not to make pronouncements.

"Now"—Red Sky wanted to know something else—"does your leg hurt too much to run more?"

The boy smiled and shook his head.

"Good. Gray Wolf is going to run ahead of us along the trail. I would like to run with you, to see how you could run from a wolf. Can you show me how fast you can run? I also want Gray Wolf to listen and see how close you can get without him hearing you. If you can get so close to a buck that you can watch him for a time then you must be a very quiet runner—well, we have already seen that. But, if you can catch a wolf and a deer then you must be fast too. I'll follow, but don't wait for me if I am too slow." The hunter smiled inwardly at this; he didn't really think that the boy could outrun him.

The two of them waited together while Gray Wolf got a head start.

After about a finger of time, Red Sky asked if the boy was ready. The boy nodded and, at the hunter's signal, started running. Red Sky was impressed by the boy's initial speed, and even more by his stealth; the hunter could not hear him at all. He stayed with the boy briefly but soon learned that he had just been warming up. Finally, the boy blazed ahead at his normal full speed and the hunter was soon left far behind.

After just a short time, the boy saw where Gray Wolf would be likely hiding, and, for fun, he left the trail and moved through the brush to touch him on the shoulder from behind as he passed by. The older hunter yelled in surprise, but then called for the boy to come back.

A while later, Red Sky joined them. The two hunters looked at the boy with strange eyes as if they couldn't believe what they had seen. But then Gray Wolf clapped him on the back, half smiling, and told him that they would meet him back in the village.

Happy to be released, the boy sped off, gaining speed as he disappeared. The two hunters started their own jog back home, slowly; they wanted to be able to speak as they traveled, to understand if each had seen the same things.

When the hunters arrived at the village they saw the boy sitting near the Long Lodge. He looked as though he'd been back for a while. The elders were waiting with him, speaking with one another and asking the boy questions about what he liked to do in the forest, and about his life in the village. The boy answered respectfully, but mostly kept quiet.

Gray Wolf asked if the boy would wait in his shelter while they spoke with the elders. Red Sky watched the boy go with his usual slow village shamble. He shook his head at the difference in the way the boy moved here.

"Well," Great Storm began, "what did you learn?"

"It's all true," Red Sky answered, shaking his head again. "The signs are all there; the fight happened just as he described it. More than that, the boy moves like a ghost in the forest—a very fast ghost. He is almost impossible to hear, very difficult to track, and I'd need to be a wolf to keep up with him."

The men related all the things they had seen and the tests they had given the boy.

"We knew he must be very fast. He's certainly an unusual boy," Great Storm said, pausing as if he were thinking—although he and the other elders had already decided what to do. "I think it's time to find a name for him, something other than boy, and he has been alone far too long. He will need to learn how to use more than just a small flint knife if he is to be a hunter. Gray Wolf, will you continue to take responsibility for his training and at the same time make sure that Dark Sun fulfills his duty to help the boy?"

Gray Wolf nodded that he would.

"I will help too, if Gray Wolf allows," Red Sky offered. "I was proud when he credited me with his knowledge of tracking. His skill is exceptional; in time I think he will be able to track the north wind."

"We will have a naming ceremony tomorrow night," said Great Storm. "Gray Wolf, as the one responsible for the boy, he will belong to your lodge and will be your son."

Gray Wolf nodded. The old hunter seemed pleased to be chosen and wondered what name the elders would give him. Normally, the mother would have much to say in the matter. But the boy had no mother, at least no living mother, and he was already almost a hunter.

Gray Wolf stopped at another shelter briefly, and then joined the boy at his own home. He explained that the boy was to become his son and that he and Red Sky would train him as a tracker, as a hunter, and as a weapon maker.

"Tomorrow night, the elders will give you a name."

The boy looked down to hide his face for a long moment, then into Gray Wolf's eyes, nodding and not yet able to speak.

"Will you join us now?" Gray Wolf said, speaking to someone outside. The boy looked towards the door and Dark Sun entered the shelter. There was a blank expression on his face; he was finding it hard to look the boy in the eye.

"If you will agree, I would like to help with your training too, even though I am only a new hunter. Sometimes the older men forget how much we need to learn. I think I can be helpful, but I will understand if you don't want me to be around you after the terrible things I said. I'm very sorry for how I treated you; I should have realized how difficult it was for you."

The boy stood and tentatively grasped Dark Sun's forearm. "We start new life today together."

The young hunter looked down at first, thanking the boy, and paused. Finally, he looked directly into the boy's eyes, as if for the first time. "I am Dark Sun, hunter of the Eldest Village. I hope to know your name soon." And with that the young hunter asked to be excused and returned to his lone vigil, but his steps were lighter now.

For The People, any opportunity to hold a celebration was a welcome change of pace. It was especially enjoyable to have a naming ceremony. A feast would be needed. Venison, bison, and an assortment of smaller game had all been hunted recently and were being cooked in fire pits and leather cauldrons, along with roots and other foods gathered by the people. Cakes sweetened with the sap from maple trees and other delicacies were being made. And there was a special drink the elders prepared that would be shared. Everyone in the village felt the excitement. and everyone seemed to know now that the boy's story was true.

It was getting late in the hunting season, and before long everyone would be eating dried foods that had been stored for the winter. These would only be supplemented occasionally by fresh meat, since hunting would be more difficult.

People were speculating about what the boy's name would be. Three Wolves was a favorite, along with Wolf Slayer, and certainly Deer Brother had a strong contingent of supporters—this last would probably also be used as a nickname, no matter what the elders said. But the elders were silent and had spent most of the night in the Long Lodge discussing the matter.

That evening, Gray Wolf approached the elders on behalf of the boy to request that Dark Sun be allowed to attend the naming ceremony. The three old men looked surprised, but immediately agreed to the request. This had been Gray Wolf's suggestion, and the boy had agreed, seeing the wisdom of it right away. The old man hoped to seal the breach and to put the whole matter behind them soon.

During the past two days, the three wolf hides had been worked and dried and worked again by a group of girls and women enlisted by Wild Flower. They were still going through the long, iterative process of drying and working the skins to keep them supple. When not being worked, they were on display for the ceremony, each stretched across an X-shaped frame made from branches. The trophies belonged to the boy and, because of the story that went with them, were much admired by everyone in the village. The boy had said these were to be gifts, but had not yet said who would receive them.

At dusk the following day, people gathered around the large communal fire at the center of the village. Food had been prepared and everything was ready. People had been finding excuses to pass near the center all afternoon; they were ready for a celebration. The boy was brought from Gray Wolf's tent and asked to stand before the elders. Great Storm stood with the three wolf hides behind him as he spoke.

"Boy, the people welcomed you into our village more than seven years ago. We didn't know who your people were at the time, and, although we sent runners to learn what we could, we didn't find anything. We discovered, much later, that a village of people who lived at the edge of the forest had been destroyed, its people murdered. It wasn't much information. We believe that your people and our people are distantly related, but we never did learn who attacked your village, or why.

"Since you never spoke, we were not sure if you had been harmed or what your condition might be, but we wanted to make sure you had a home. We hoped for a long time that your people would come for you, but it was strange to us that you liked to spend so much of your time alone in the forest. Now it seems that the time spent there has been good for you and for the village.

"We want to complete your welcome as one of The People today—you will be an important part of the village, a hunter. It seems you have the skill to one day become a great hunter, and maybe we have as much to learn from you as you do from us.

While the village is your home, we recognize that the forest is also a special place for you and we want to acknowledge this."

The older hunter joined the boy at the fire as the elder was speaking.

"Gray Wolf, will you accept this boy into your shelter as your son?"

"Yes, I accept him," the hunter replied formally.

Great Storm looked at the boy. "From this time Gray Wolf is your father and from this day you will have a new name. You are Forest Shadow. We believe that you are drawn to the forest for a reason. The men say that you move through the forest like a ghost and, from what we see, the wolves could only try to catch a shadow." The old man looked at the three wolf hides on display as he said this. There were chuckles from the people watching.

"The village is stronger today than it was yesterday. We ask that you allow your strength, and elusiveness, to be added to the village, and in your time you will be asked to pass your skills along to others, just as the people are passing along their skills to you."

Great Storm then took an ancient knife from a soft leather pouch. It was an heirloom from the depths of time, primitive and obviously never intended to have a handle, but it was still very sharp.

"This is the knife of my father's father's father, from so many generations back that none can remember when it came to be. This blade has been passed down to the chief elder of the Eldest Village since we became The People." The chief stepped forward and pierced the boy's arm with the sacred blade. A few drops of his blood were collected in a wooden bowl and mixed in a liquid from a large water skin made from the stomach of a bison, then it was mixed back in with the remaining liquid.

"We are The People and so that all will know this, we will share a part of you with the naming drink as we welcome you. Everyone will share the drink of brotherhood and greet our newest member!"

The boy spoke quietly to the old man, asking him something that seemed important.

"Yes, Forest Shadow. You may give your gifts now." Everyone's interest piqued again; all were wondering who would receive the three hides.

"I want Father, Gray Wolf, to have first hide—the first hide for my first friend." Everyone had been sure the older man would receive one. Gray Wolf nodded his thanks.

"The second fur is for Morning Song." There was some laughter in the crowd that startled the boy.

The elder saw his confusion and tried to help. "Morning Song, I think you can accept this as a gift of friendship, without a deeper meaning. Forest Shadow doesn't know all of the intricacies of our customs and understandably sees you as someone he can trust. Will you accept it in this spirit?"

"Yes," the girl said, blushing. "Forest Shadow is my friend and I will try to help him understand the customs."

The elder looked at the boy again, and everyone wondered who was left. Forest Shadow took a deep breath; he had been practicing what he was going to say all day.

"When my village killed, woman, I think mother, carry me to the forest to save. My old life ended, my new life started. Now another new life starts. New father. New friends. Today is new life. I ask that new friend, Dark Sun, accept third wolf hide from Forest Shadow."

The choice surprised everyone, including the elder. After a long pause, the older boy stepped forward and said that he too would accept the hide as a token of their new friendship. The elder looked at the boy who was now Forest Shadow from the corners of his eyes, wondering if this had actually been the boy's idea, or Gray Wolf's.

"Let's begin the feast." These were words everyone had been waiting to hear.

One by one each member of the village came to receive their part of the sacred drink, a kind of wine fermented from native fruits—it also contained other herbs that remained a secret known only to the elders. The drink held spiritual significance and the recipe was another of the legacies from their distant past. While strong, the wine was only mildly intoxicating, and only a small amount was given to each member of the village. The herbs contained other attributes that allowed people to see visions. But that night the concentration was very mild. The elders reserved strong concentrations for other, much different ceremonies.

Everyone drank from the skin and then went to place their hand on Forest Shadow's shoulder as they said the words that the boy had waited seven years to hear: "Welcome, Forest Shadow, welcome, brother."

There was an abundance of food of different kinds, and the people stayed up very late celebrating their newest member.

EPILOGUE

Forest Shadow sat in front of his father, Gray Wolf, who was now the chief village elder. The elder listened to his son describe the hunt that he would lead to the west, far across the plains.

Gray Wolf absentmindedly played with his new grandson as he listened to his son talk. He noted that the infant had his father's eyes. The old man was anxious to see if the boy had inherited some of Forest Shadow's spirit as well.

The hunter looked at his newborn son sitting in the lap of his father. The old man's contentment with and captivation by the infant was obvious. Gray Wolf and Forest Shadow still shared the same shelter, together with Morning Song and the baby, who had yet to be named. It was good that the old man had come to have a second family so late in life; even a village elder needed people to take care of him.

Forest Shadow still liked to run in the forest and still sought the peacefulness of the early-morning fog. Even now, if he allowed it to happen, his mind would return to those last minutes of his first life, to his mother carrying her young son to the edge of the forest, praying that he would survive to find a new life somewhere. The hunter hoped she was able to see him now from her place beyond the world and to know that her final struggle had not been in vain.

The End

CPSIA information can be obtained at www.ICGtesting.com
Printed in the USA
BVOW07s0155181214

379946BV00001B/4/P